AF124960

Gerold Trank, a thirty-nine year old historian, works as secretary of the renowned Swiss 'Foundation for the Propagation of Humanistic Ideals'. Founded over one hundred and fifty years ago and funded by commerce and industry, the organization supports traditional – and only traditional – cultural activities.

During one particular board meeting Trank is overwhelmed by a flood of thoughts. He realizes in desperation that his life is slipping away pointlessly. Torn between conformity and rebellion, between finding reasons for his present existence and dreaming of escape scenarios, he finally finds a way out that surprises even himself.

Andreas Pritzker, born in 1945, is a Swiss physicist and author. He has published the following texts: *Filberts Verhängnis* (novel, 1990), *Das Ende der Täuschung* (novel, 1993), *Eingeholte Zeit* (narrative, 2001), *Die Anfechtungen des Juan Zinniker* (novel, 2007), *Allenthalben Lug und Trug* (novel, 2010), *Geschichte des SIN* (science history, 2013). He also co-edited a number of oral history texts.

Andreas Pritzker

Time Reclaimed

A Narrative

Translated from the German by
Alex Gabriel

Originally published in German as *Eingeholte Zeit* by munda, Brugg (Switzerland), in 2001

Translated from the German by Alex Gabriel

Produced and published by
BoD – Books on Demand, Norderstedt (Germany)

ISBN: 978-3-7357-5687-9

More books by Andreas Pritzker
are presented on
www.munda.ch

FSC
www.fsc.org

MIX
Papier aus verantwortungsvollen Quellen
Paper from responsible sources
FSC® C105338

1

The spacious room is plastered white; its carpeting is dove grey. The empty walls bring to mind a cinema screen, while the carpet is reminiscent of the stone slabs of an ancient Roman forum. The stucco on the ceiling dates from the time the mansion was built. It features intertwined ribbons of flowers, which appear almost as living natural blossoms that have been frozen into the dead plaster by some sort of curse.

In the center of the room is a white glazed oak table, twenty-four feet long. It is surrounded by burgundy-upholstered chairs with chrome-plated tubular steel frames. Several times each year, a group of distinguished men spends the day together at this table, carrying out its established rituals. The men spread papers across the table – papers full of ideas and thoughts – and engage in heated debates. Today is one such day.

Everything in the room seems to fit together perfectly, although the various aspects of its décor were not planned together at any single point in time. The new chairs, for instance, were selected by the current chairman. The table, the carpeting, and the white walls, however, remain from the times of his predecessors. So does the painting – the only one present – that dominates the front of the room. The design seems to have emerged at random, yet, at the same time, it quite clearly has been guided by an established frame of reference.

The room is very bright thanks to a row of high windows, which also provide a panoramic view over the city. It is just as the mansion's builder had envisioned: far from the common people – from the tradesmen and the blue-collar workers and the subsistence-seekers

– avoiding direct contact with the masses, while still being able to keep an eye on everything.

The caretaker has opened the windows early this morning, just as he does each day that a meeting will be held here. The summer morning air, brisk and fresh, now wafts freely through the room. The caretaker has also set out sealed bottles of sparkling water – a local Swiss brand – which stand in formation on the table like soldiers reporting for duty. The sparkling water is accompanied by sparkling-clean glasses, upside-down, their invitingly pristine brims resting against the table.

Three ashtrays have been arranged upon the table as well. Bearing the logo of a major Swiss brewery, they seem somewhat out-of-place here. But there is a story – an earlier ashtray-related misadventure – behind their presence here. There was only one ashtray here at the time, an expensive crystal piece, which Oederlein always used to appropriate for his own use. On one occasion, when Berglass needed to empty the blackened ash from his pipe, Oederlein thrust the ashtray so forcefully in his direction that it careened over the edge of the table and shattered in a million pieces. Brockstätte then ordered Trank to have the caretaker procure sufficient ashtrays so that they could avoid such incidents in the future. But when he first laid his eyes upon the garish advertising pieces, Brockstätte immediately grimaced and blurted out derisively, "What is this place supposed to be, some kind of neighborhood bar?" Right at that very moment, though, Oederlein entered the room and saw the new ashtrays; he took one of them in his hands and, caressing it tenderly with his stubby fingers, praised Brockstätte for his good taste. Oederlein explained that, while he usually preferred red wine, this brewery was simply the finest; he deigned to drink beer from no other.

Gerold Trank, Ph.D., is the first to enter the room today, as usual. With his dove grey suit and his burgundy tie, he seems to comprise an extension of the décor of the room itself. He shivers and heads straight towards the windows, shuts them, and wishes he could just stand there and simply enjoy the view. When the weather is beautiful, it always does a number on him. The cityscapes in the bright morning light... the fertile, yellow-green fields... the blue sea... views like these lead him on, make him believe that there is a beautiful reality hidden somewhere far, far away from his own dreary daily routine. A yearning desire is awakened deep inside him, yet he is simultaneously instilled with an unsettling feeling that, for him, this beautiful reality is simply unattainable.

Everyone, incidentally, heads straight towards those windows when they first enter the room, and declares that the view is absolutely magnificent. Everyone who is not completely blind – even those who never occupy themselves with anything beyond the usual – digestion, money, sexual desire. It's well enough; too much gazing into the distance can make a person lose himself too easily.

Trank is already accustomed to brushing aside his yearning. After all, he has duties to fulfill – every day, including today. He examines the huge tape recorder on the table. Then he tests the powerful overhead projector. Are there enough colored pens? Check. A spare bulb in the drawer? Check again. Good.

* * *

This is all extremely important, of course. Once, for example, the projector's bulb flickered out right in the middle of a discourse by Oederlein, a member of the

9

Swiss National Council, as well as owner and president of a thriving, well-known chemical factory. And there was no spare bulb.

Chairman Biland frowned and leaned back in his chair. Brockstätte promptly dashed across the room and rifled through the drawer. Nope, no spare bulb. "Mr. Chairman, my distinguished gentlemen," Oederlein declared stiffly, "I have put great efforts into preparing my presentation, and I quite simply cannot proceed without the use of the projector."

His speech, as Trank would forever remember, dealt with "the provision of cultural resources to Alpine valley populations with narrow horizons." Oederlein was just about to project, onto the white wall of the room, some slides related to an educational program that had been developed in conjunction with local clergy. And why local clergy, rather than local educational professionals? That is exactly what Oederlein was just getting ready to explain, when the bulb died.

"Mr. Oederlein, I apologize. I deeply regret this situation," said the chairman, who then glanced at Trank, hunched down behind the tape recorder, and demanded: "Get us a spare bulb immediately; you yourself can figure out how. Make it quick, chop-chop."

So Trank sprang to his feet and hurried to find the caretaker, who was not in his quarters. Trank finally found him with a technician in the boiler room, thanks to the clanging noises that rattled up through the stairwell. "Excuse me, it's extremely urgent," gasped Trank.

Not as far as the caretaker was concerned though. "In a minute!" he grunted, then slowly re-lit his cigar and continued fiddling with the boiler, along with the smirking technician.

Trank was already envisioning having to rush over to the adjacent schoolhouse to beg for a bulb, when the caretaker finally decided to come up from the cellar. He rummaged through a closet in his quarters, and finally emerged with the right box. He determinedly pushed past Trank, and marched on ahead of him towards the meeting room.

The debate there at the moment concerned the question of whether the primary culpability for such mishaps lay in the inadequacies of the equipment or of the staff.

The caretaker replaced the bulb unhurriedly, re-lit his cigar once again, and left the room. The chairman thanked him effusively as he exited; Brockstätte waved in his direction as well.

Trank knew that the question of responsibility would inevitably come back to him now. He saw it coming, and it troubled him. But deep inside, he always felt responsible anyway.

"This is the last time," the chairman said to Trank, "that I will allow such a silly oversight to occur here. Not because 'time is money'; we have chosen to be here of our own accord. But for just that very reason, I expect you to be prudent in this regard. I hold you responsible for making sure that our meetings can take place without such disturbances."

Everyone seated around the table nodded, except Hartmann, who hunched down over his files.

But wasn't the spare bulb a matter for the caretaker? For a brief moment Trank agonized over the idea that it would be tougher to replace someone with practical experience in maintaining boilers and supervising cleaning ladies than it would be to replace a foundation secretary. There were tons of other Ph.D.'s who would simply jump at the chance for a position such as his.

* * *

The weather is magnificent this morning, but Gerold Trank is suffering from stomach pain. The cause of the pain is unknown. It may even be his heart, according to what he has read. The pain has taken control over Trank's bowels, just as firmly as life has taken control over Trank himself. In this condition, human contact is the last thing he wants. He craves only a long, lonely coastline with panoramic views of endless, timeless waves. The waves would certainly be able to wash his pain away.

At the moment however, his mind must focus on his duties as second secretary of the Foundation for the Propagation of Humanistic Ideals. The precise nature of the foundation is not obvious from its official name – it is only when Trank states that he works for the "FPHI" that people nod in comprehension.

The first member of the foundation's board to enter the room is Professor Berglass, its representative from the academic world – a hulking six-foot-three, balding, with a fringe of grey hair, a bulbous nose, and a gently flowing full beard. His rimless glasses make him look intelligent; if only they could actually make him intelligent! Berglass is, to be perfectly frank, a blatherer. A man with a seemingly unlimited supply of time. When Berglass holds the floor, he rambles on and on and on – never for less than ten minutes. And when he is finally done, no one has any idea what his point actually was.

Berglass is always the first board member to show up; that's the only way he can assure himself of securing his coveted seat. He now sits down ponderously near the head of the table, right beside the seat of the chairman. When Trank approaches him, he stands up just as ponderously and shakes Trank's hand for what seems like an eternity. He complains about the summer heat that will almost certainly manifest itself over the course of the day, about the sluggish traffic in the city, and about the hassle of finding a parking spot. These days every shopgirl and secretary has her own car, he grumbles; it's no wonder the streets are clogged. For the most part, Berglass does not look Trank in the eye as he is speaking; he is too busy keeping an eye on the door. When Hartmann enters, Berglass breaks off his bitter social commentary and turns to greet him.

Trank heads back towards his usual spot at the foot of the table, a space he shares with the tape recorder.

Hartmann, a trade union secretary by profession, eventually turns away from Berglass to greet Trank. A conspiratorial look briefly flashes across his face in the process; his expression makes it clear that he regards Trank as having a lower social status.

Every trade union secretary seems to be either very fat or very thin, Trank has found – never in between. In Hartmann's case, it is the former. He sits down near Berglass, who has been waiting for him this whole time with an outstretched hand and a somewhat silly grin, and who once again starts going on about the summer weather, the sluggish traffic in the city, and the hassle of finding a parking spot, this time leaving aside his displeasure at the growing number of female com-muters whose cars clog up the roads. Still, his diatribe does not inspire even the slightest trace of sympathy in Hartmann; the latter is a former railway official, quite proud of the fact that he does not own a car.

One after another, the other board members arrive. They are all men who are getting on in years, dressed in such a refined manner, on the whole, that Professor Berglass' corduroy suit, originally custom-tailored but now entirely shapeless, and Hartmann's black leather jacket both seem completely out-of-place. Hands are shaken all around the table – fine, soft hands that have signed many a signature. Chairman Biland enters together with Brockstätte, who asks Trank – loud enough to be heard above the commotion in the room – whether he has, in fact, checked everything out thoroughly. Oederlein is the last to arrive, greeting everyone – everyone besides Trank, that is.

The chairman now pulls a silver pen from his breast pocket, and starts to tap the table with it deliberately. The chatter subsides, and all heads in the room turn towards him as if drawn by some invisible force. Only then does he begin to speak: "Gentlemen, I am notoriously strict when it comes to starting meetings on schedule. When necessary, I have even been known to commence a meeting with no other attendees present; fortunately, thanks to your commendable punctuality, it will not be necessary for me to do so today." He delivers the same line at every meeting. And every time, the board members respond with the obligatory smiles; Trank finds it absolutely cringe-worthy. "I am glad," the chairman continues, "that we have all managed to be present today, as we are here to discuss an important matter, namely our contributions to the celebration of the 700-year anniversary of the Swiss Confederation."

Trank has already pressed all the necessary buttons on the tape recorder. The level indicator's oscillations testify to the fact that the chairman's words are, in fact, being registered and preserved in the chromium dioxide. Out of sheer habit, Trank has also noted the names of those present, using shorthand abbreviations that he came up with himself. B&B stands for Biland and Brockstätte, a B with an apostrophe is for Berglass, and VW is for von Warteck; Oederlein is an O with a line through it, though he sometimes writes out Oed; he likewise abbreviates Kindlimann as Kind; and while he originally shortened Hartmann to Hart, he later switched to a simple meaningless H.

* * *

Trank remembers how, on his first day of work, Brockstätte had ceremoniously assigned him the responsibility of keeping minutes, solemnly urging him not to take the task lightly. "Always remember that the minutes of each meeting, which will bear your signature for as long as you work at the foundation, are stored in a secure repository and will serve as a valuable resource for future historians." And Brockstätte had further stressed the importance of taking notes despite the presence of the tape recorder – even the best of technologies can malfunction, and you simply never know when it might happen.

Up until his eleventh meeting, Trank had complied with these directives in an exemplary manner. Today is his twenty-seventh meeting, and he can attest to the fact that the tape recorder, a top-quality Swiss model, has never failed him. And that's not the only fact that renders his note-taking entirely superfluous. By now, he knows every detail of the foundation's dealings better than anyone else. After all, he had prepared the agenda items under the watchful eye of Brockstätte, who had a penchant for rampaging through Trank's drafts, ruthlessly and mercilessly attacking each page with a red pen. Over the years, Trank has gotten to know the minutiae of the board members' tendencies extremely well. At this point, based on past experience, he can accurately predict what each one will say. And when he will say it. And even how he will say it.

Trank could write the minutes of the meeting even if he weren't actually present – or, indeed, even if the meeting itself did not actually take place.

But, oh, what a scandal it would be if the tape recorder were to break down and if he were to find himself without notes. Chairman Biland, who claims to be able to conclusively judge a person's character based on a single test – and who still clearly remembers the projector bulb episode – would write him off forever as a lazy, irresponsible, cynical slacker. And Brockstätte, standing beside the chairman's desk, would exclaim, "Such an incident has never occurred in the entire history of the foundation, since it was founded back in 1833. We must repeat the entire meeting, there is simply no other choice, and I am even afraid that Oederlein and von Warteck may immediately resign. What a shame!"

Trank's eleventh meeting coincided with a bout of pure loathing for the world. Even though he himself did not fully understand where it came from, it allowed him to liberate himself somewhat from his burden. He valiantly decided to no longer dutifully record the details of the minutes during each meeting. Since then, he has just scribbled coded messages about the men present, or other personal notes. Occasionally, when the shopping list that Maria dictated to him that day was once again forgotten on the kitchen table, he attempts to recreate it during the meeting.

It feels good to set himself free through his acts of hidden defiance, despite – or perhaps precisely because of – the fact that such disobedience does not come naturally to him. In fact, it gives him very conflicting emotions, a circumstance that he chalks up to his strict Catholic upbringing. He feels guilty; yet, at the same time, he derives a certain acute pleasure from the rebellious actions.

* * *

Chairman Biland opens a bottle of sparkling water, fills his glass, and takes a sip. Trank admires his calculated movements, and watches the bubbles make their way to the surface. Biland stifles a small burp, and inquires as to whether anyone has any comments on the minutes of the previous meeting.

Professor Berglass quickly raises his hand. Far be it from him to be pedantic, he says, but the secretary appears to have made a silly little error in the previous meeting's minutes; unfortunately, this could potentially lead to some misunderstanding, even if only in the distant future. While referencing Mr. Oederlein's enlightening statements, he says, at the bottom of page two, Mr. Trank appears to have accidentally written "National Counsel" instead of "National Council"; in order to avoid confusion, the matter should be corrected.

The chairman nods in Trank's direction. Trank looks down at his papers – not because of anything written on them, but rather to hide the expression of disgust that has surfaced on his face. He jots down his doctor's telephone number, resolving to make a call later today about his stomachache.

The meeting proceeds. Trank sits there, trapped and helpless. Time passes like the beating of his heart – slow, lethargically slow. He has absolutely no interest in what is being said; it is no different from when his parents made him attend mass as a child. Inevitably, his mind wanders away from the meeting, and his thoughts begin to flow, just as they used to flow in the gloomy, incense-filled church long ago.

* * *

The constant, pervasive flow of thoughts is a curse; it is like a flood of biblical proportions. He is incapable of suppressing it. He cannot even slow it down. When his body sits still, his mind just gets going. It happens during his agonizingly sleepless nights as well. He is engulfed by a deluge, an overwhelming torrent of thoughts, which surge towards the surface. As if the thoughts have flowed from some inexhaustible spring deep inside him, into an overflowing reservoir.

He has tried to overcome this problem with meditation exercises that Tibetan monks use to completely empty their minds. The exercises didn't work for him; he wasn't surprised. After all, his life could not possibly be more completely different from the life of a Tibetan monk. His thoughts are the thoughts of a thirty-nine-year-old married Swiss man with a Ph.D. in history. A man with two children who are growing up fast, and a townhouse in the countryside, twelve miles from the city limits – it's tiny, but he owns it free and clear. And he also has the car of his dreams, a Saab 900 Turbo, whose completely unnecessary extra horsepower he relishes whenever he drives it.

Trank has left the car at home today; there are simply too few parking spots behind the mansion where the meeting is taking place. And, of course, they are reserved for the board members who are deemed to most warrant them. One is for Oederlein, of course, as a member of the National Council. And another one for von Warteck, CEO and President of the General Life Insurance Company. And another for Major General Kindlimann. But there is none for Professor Berglass; he would have loved to be able to park here, but could not convince Brockstätte. And there would be none for Hartmann even if he had a car.

But none of this matters to Gerold Trank right now. He floats aimlessly in his web of thoughts, not knowing what he really wants. He knows only that something, something, is tormenting him deep inside, and that he needs to finally figure out what on earth it is. He is confident that the compass of his soul will guide him, and will show him the right path.

For now, he is comforted by the thought that he is not the only one who hangs in this sort of limbo. On this very summer morning, with the sun shining brightly, there must be hundreds of people out there in the city thinking about how miserable they are and wondering how they might turn their lives around. Probably some of them have stomachaches as well, just like him. They may have already tried some sort of cure, which likely didn't help much; maybe baking soda, or a glass of Alpenbitter. His own doctor, on the other hand, had advised him, "Just breathe deeply twenty times, and focus on the pain."

Instead, he allows his mind to wander. The painting hanging behind the chairman, directly across from Trank, is quite colorful and extremely large – he guesses about eight feet by twelve feet. It covers almost an entire wall of the bright room. Trank is constantly transfixed by the painting. A nude woman traipses from the left of the scene towards the right, in lush, verdant natural surroundings; she has a cornucopia in her arms, a triumphant expression on her face, and a swelling in her womb. The very depiction of motherhood, flush with fertility. The image strikes Trank as the embodiment of a sort of moral plea, and yet this morning, without knowing why, he feels strangely repulsed by the sober, unerotic, humorless scene.

But is there really nothing he can do about this? There is something he can do, of course. A warm, feminine body emerges from his imagination, lolling on the table in front of him. She is a blend of some women he has known (including his wife Maria and his occasional mistress Elisabeth), with others that he has only seen. He contemplates the creature's radiant, shimmering, satiny skin... the smiling curve of her upper lip against her teeth... the contour of her knee... and all those other little details that inevitably cause him to immediately fall passionately in love with her whole being. The delectable bulge of her two full breasts when she lies on her back, their perkiness when she sits up. Her delicately curved hips, framing a neatly trimmed triangle, the holy grail.

"This is real," he thinks, "and the meeting is illusory. It is taking place in an imaginary world, a world in which I would likely perish from a lack of eroticism and humor. "

And where have the humor and eroticism in his life gone? He thinks back to ten or twelve years ago, the intense attraction between himself and Maria, which manifested itself not only in their sizzling sex life, but also in their playful and witty banter. All that is no more now. His entire existence has become oppressively dull. Even his adventures with Elisabeth have now become solemn affairs. Deep down, he believes that humor and eroticism are true art forms, that they are what make life liveable – and with a combination of the two, even more so. Many medieval tales were essentially based on an interconnection between humor and eroticism – and no one knows this better than Trank, a specialist in medieval history.

Wait a second, stop. That's all in the past, a different lifetime. He has long ago abandoned that career path.

Dr. Gerold Trank is no longer a historian these days, he is a secretary – a secretary in a morbidly serious institution that could not possibly incorporate any less humor or eroticism.

* * *

Meanwhile, the board is busy discussing the new application form. The chairman's youngest daughter, a bright young woman, has designed it on her computer. She studies art history, and thus has the final say with regard to layout as far as the chairman is concerned. The foundation has paid her handsomely for her work. Trank knows this because Brockstätte, generally cautious with regard to such matters, instructed Trank to sign the check instead of himself.

The FPHI logo is emblazoned across the top of the form. Beneath it, in bold letters, is one sentence: "Every Swissman in possession of civil rights may request assistance from the Foundation for any purposes that are consistent with humanistic ideals."

The female secretaries at the foundation put up a big fuss. They were united in their demand that Swisswomen be specifically mentioned as well. Brockstätte dismissed the idea. "In this context, it is quite clear that the word 'Swissman' covers women as well," he asserted. "We're lucky there aren't any women on the board," he later cackled to Trank when they were alone, "or else we'd all have to sit through a huge debate about this."

The men are, in fact, in the middle of a huge debate right now. Should an applicant be required to state his military grade and rank, as Major General Kindlimann insists? And identify his employer, as von Warteck, the corporate executive, contends? And list two references from public figures, as National Council member Oederlein feels is absolutely essential?

* * *

Trank dreads the very idea of documenting these details in the meeting minutes. And what for anyway? After a hundred and sixty years of shrewd adaptation, the foundation serves only one purpose: it basically acts as a bank. When Trank joined FPHI, Brockstätte explained the process. "Our state's coffers are over-flowing, you see. Of course the big companies don't want to cram them even more full, so they try to avoid paying taxes whenever possible. But still, they continue to have patriotic mindsets, so they donate large sums of money to us, and we use this money to finance youth sports camps, archery contests, traditional wrestling tournaments, traveling exhibitions about our heroic ancestors, musical events, local history reports that duly honor our past, etcetera."

All things that fall nicely in line with the established order, thinks Trank. He has almost resigned himself to accepting the power of the established order – yet as a historian, he also recognizes that change is simply inherent in this world.

And that things only change when the course of history dictates it – never before such time. He believes that people are fundamentally wrong when they think that they have control over historical developments, and that they can effect change all by themselves. Rather, it is the historical developments themselves, in fact, that have far more control over people. The most that people can do is compliantly go along the predetermined path like ants following a trail, rather than trying to resist. Everything happens as it does thanks to the mechanisms of historical developments.

Unfortunately, historical developments determine not only the fate of mankind, but also the fate of individual men such as himself, Gerold Trank. Still, he draws hope from an analogy to the world of physics, in which a single molecule has more leeway than the object of which it is a part.

But how much leeway does he actually have?

The forces that shape people's lives operate in obscure and incomprehensible ways. These forces have made him second secretary at FPHI, probably forever, while they have made Brockstätte first secretary – clearly a good place to start, there could be no debate about that. The careers of Biland, von Warteck, and Oederlein all started in a similar fashion.

There was a time when Trank tried to understand these things from a historical perspective. Secretly researching in the Historical and Biographical Dictionary of Switzerland, he discovered that Biland, the foundation's chairman, came from a prestigious Swiss dynastic family. He found a Federal Councilor Biland, high ranking military personnel, three generations of businessmen, and even a few clergymen.

With an indulgent smile on his face, he quickly rejected the notion of a firm oligarchical grip on the country that thwarted the rise of any outsiders. He had encountered an army of social climbers that repudiated this theory. Some of them, in fact, sat on the foundation's board.

Professor Berglass, for example. At first he treated Trank with a sort of careful deference. Later he realized that the status of the second secretary was far below his own, and suddenly a nasty tone crept into his voice whenever it was directed at Trank.

Even Oederlein, now member of the National Council, had to climb to get there. A country boy from humble roots, who used to spend two hours each morning, even in the dead of winter, walking to his school up the next valley. His difficult past sometimes echoes in his voice when the board engages in critical discussions of the current prosperity.

This was not the case, though, for Major General Kindlimann, descendant of one of Napoleon's own lieutenant-generals. And even less so for von Warteck, who comes from a long line of nobility.

Had the mysterious forces of life spun differently, Trank could have been a social climber as well. Professor Gerold Trank, Ph.D. – sounds nice, doesn't it? Some acquaintances who are familiar with Trank's case, and who know the workings of the academic community quite well, believe that it had not been far from becoming a reality.

For several years, while working as an assistant to the famous medieval researcher Professor Wickler, Trank had felt himself above the mundane. He had faithfully compiled bibliographies, drafted correspondence, reviewed tedious publications, and tutored foul-smelling students on behalf of his mentor. He had proudly led Wickler's seminars, and had been fortunate enough to publish thirty-one scholarly articles together with the renowned expert.

Two years before Wickler's retirement, while merry with wine at the Institute for Medieval History's Christmas party, the old man had declared Trank his likely successor, laying his greasy fur hat on Trank's head as a sort of coronation.

And Trank had believed in it.

In his incredible naiveté, he was just begging to be disappointed. The events that followed were like the end of a pregnancy. He was extricated from the warm, protective womb of his historical texts, and was thrust into the wilderness of the working world, entirely unprepared to handle the struggle for survival ahead of him.

Trank knew about much of what was happening at the time, though not the finer details. Looking back, though, it all seems so clear. Wickler, generally despised at the university, moved nearer and nearer to his end, and no longer had much of a say in matters. He made one last attempt to promote Trank's candidacy, then ditched him. He knocked on the doors of the people who mattered, and recommended a former student who was then at the Sorbonne. The nadir of it all came when he called Trank into his office, stood up behind his desk, and urged his befuddled assistant, "For the very sake of medieval history studies, just give up your candidacy for this chair and support your former colleague, or else we'll end up losing the chair to one of those damned modern historians."

Trank decided to do something beyond that. It was the only correct thing to do – as he is still convinced to this day. At the end of the semester, he simply refused to renew his semiannual contract. The dean's secretary summoned her boss, who reacted as if the world had been turned upside down. The university was besieged by scholarly applicants who lusted after its warm confines. The university always decided when one's employment there would terminate.

But Trank just left the rapidly aging, half-a-year-from-retirement Wickler sitting there helplessly, trembling from the indignity, and finally turned his back on the university.

Maria had shared in his disappointments, and now shared in his defiance. She had some savings of her own, which she had set aside for an emergency. They decided to take advantage of their unexpected new freedom to travel with the children for as long as the money would allow.

They spent a few months relaxing on the island of Belle-Île, off the rugged coast of Brittany. Trank fell in love with the island's reddish rocks and the deep green of the sea.

Maria, one-quarter Breton, had relatives on the island. It was their second stay there; the first had been on their honeymoon, among the throngs of summer vacationers.

Now they were visiting during the windy days of April, with dazzling white cloud formations drifting across the luscious blue sky, and the high season rush still far away. Maria's relatives had left them a seafront cottage with two small, bright, salty-smelling rooms, in which they lived somewhat primitively while spending practically nothing. It seemed like they would stay there forever. Time drifted onward like the clouds through the sky.

Trank sometimes got the feeling that, even now, he was still living off the vitality of those months.

One breezy summer day, when he popped into the town of Le Palais to pick up the mail that Maria's mother had forwarded, he found that he was being drawn back into the clutches of the working world. His application for employment in the position of second secretary at the renowned Foundation for the Propagation of Humanistic Ideals – an application that had been prepared and dispatched on the exact same day that he left the university behind, without any particular expectations – had been answered.

When the envelope with FPHI's insignia had arrived, Maria's anxious mother, full of respect for everything institutional, had forwarded it via express mail. In a surprisingly warm tone, the letter said that the foundation considered itself fortunate that such a noted young historian was interested in the position. He was welcome to present himself for an interview whenever it would be convenient for him, ideally as soon as possible. It was signed by the foundation's chairman.

Trank's wounded heart was moved. The chairman was specifically welcoming him as a historian, which showed a certain regard for the field, a respect similar to that which Trank himself still harbored. Standing there at the post office, he started dreaming. Maybe he could at least partially make up for the loss of his academic position, and continue to pursue some amount of research. In his mind, he saw himself boldly approaching the chairman and offering to write a comprehensive history of the foundation.

He was unaware, at the time, that all such correspondence was actually written by the chairman's secretary, who understood people remarkably well, as only a woman in her position could. And she managed to write exactly what she knew they would want to hear, yet without it sounding forced. The perfect way to lure them in.

Trank, nevertheless, was feeling glum when he returned to the cottage. He found Maria there in old jeans and a baggy sweater, her black hair pulled back in a ponytail, standing at the stove and preparing a soup. In that moment, he found her especially lovely. He paused in the doorway, feeling thousands of invisible threads binding him to this woman. She turned around and smiled at him. Just like when they had first met, at a campground on Lake Biel.

Trank, after finishing his studies, had been on his

way to the south of France in his Citroën, while Maria had been staying for a few days with her brother and his wife, who were spending their summer vacation by the lake. Sparks flew. Maria packed her bag without a second thought and headed off with him in his car.

That was six years before Brittany – now fourteen years ago.

The time on Belle-Île brought back what they had experienced in Provence, where their lives were permanently intertwined – pine forests, overgrown ruins, the scent of lavender and of their own young bodies, the air shimmering in the heat.

These days, though, they had their children with them as well. Fortunately for Trank, his own kids are generally cheerful and calm – unlike some of the whiny little devils he has encountered elsewhere. They are very close to each other and they love to play together. He gives credit for this to Maria's serene, composed nature – certainly not to his own neurotic and volatile personality.

Maria was thrilled about the potential job at FPHI.

She foresaw a stable future with the organization, and dreamed of prestige and of a higher salary. The children were just as thrilled. Although the island had much to offer them, Trank realized, their life there lacked variety. They wanted to go back to the life they lived before, to their friends, to their grandparents.

Maria's relatives on the island – grumpy, unfamiliar, and with no desire to cater to the children's needs – certainly did not fill any void in their lives. There were scattered visits to their second cousin Berthe in her filthy, messy, and sort of creepy home; the children found these visits awkward. And they also found Berthe's galettes disgusting, the stale, greasy cakes that she shoveled out of a tin canister with her gouty fingers and shoved in their faces until they finally succumbed and ate.

So, Trank drove back to Le Palais that same day and booked a spot on the next ferry.

The following day, beneath a dramatic red dawn sky, they packed their things into the Citroën, returned the keys of the cottage, and set out for home. They made it as far as the town of Vierzon that day, and stayed in a bleak, musty hotel. That morning, he and Maria woke up full of bites from some sort of critters – fleas, lice, or bedbugs, they didn't know which. Since then, Trank has always recommended anyone traveling through France to avoid stopping in Vierzon.

He nervously imagined himself showing up for the job interview with his head shaved and uncontrollable itching all over his body. But his doctor just laughed, reached for his prescription pad, and told him not to worry. He prescribed an advanced shampoo, which Trank was to use for the next three days, changing the sheets each day as well. I guarantee it'll help, said the doctor.

* * *

Major General Kindlimann ceremoniously takes the floor. He asks the board to finance the publication of a book highlighting the Swiss military leaders of the last 700 years (eighty percent of whom served foreign militaries – what a shame!)

He speaks so loud that Trank is wrenched from his thoughts and cannot help but listen. His booming voice doesn't seem to match his slender frame. According to Brockstätte, the guys in the army used to swear that Kindlimann was so thin that no enemy shooter could ever hit him.

The chairman grabs Brockstätte's elbow and murmurs something to him. Brockstätte then waves Trank over and whispers to him, "Call Mr. Hablützel – you know, the lawyer, Miss Derring has his number – and tell him that Chairman Biland wants to meet him at eleven tomorrow morning."

Trank quietly exits the room.

If the tape recorder were to fail now, there would be no record of the proceedings. What would Biland and Brockstätte say then? Nothing. Because ultimately it really doesn't matter to the two of them. They decide what constitutes a problem and what does not, Trank observes with envy, recognizing that his own place is entirely outside the sphere from which such power can be exercised over other people. Now is exactly the sort of moment in which the meeting minutes can be dispensed with. Kindlimann probably wouldn't make a fuss, even if his name never appeared in the minutes again. Except if there was a discussion of the Swiss cavalry, whose dissolution he still mourns; he had commanded one of the country's last cavalry regiments.

Trank discreetly knocks on the door of Brockstätte's secretary's office and tentatively enters. From the window there is a view of the mossy backyard, where the cars are parked in the shade of hundred-year-old trees. Kindlimann's ancient Mercedes is there, probably the same car he used in the army before scrounging it off them when he retired. There is Oederlein's Maserati, as well as Biland's large, sleek, armored Volvo. The latter seems like it would belong to von Warteck; in fact, though, the insurance company CEO drives an all-terrain jeep.

A strong personal touch is evident in Miss Derring's office. Ikebana-style flower arrangements are distributed all around the room – she clearly appears to have taken lessons. She herself is attractive and extremely well-groomed, and strikes Trank as having a certain air of refinement. He finds himself desiring to pursue an affair with her.

The idea is not really so far-fetched – he had, in fact, kept up an affair with her predecessor for about three and a half months. But only after the woman no longer worked for the foundation. There was no way that was he going to have a fling in the workplace, and especially not with Brockstätte's secretary – as a medieval specialist, he almost felt like his superior had some sort of unwritten privilege, which took precedence over his own satisfactions. And so, while Trank certainly feels aroused when he sees Miss Derring, he does not act upon it.

And, as a result, he becomes self-conscious in her presence.

He knows, incidentally, that he behaves awkwardly, floundering in a web of morality, fear, conscience, and lust. He is a skilled observer of human behavior, after all – even with regard to his own. It all has to do with his dichotomous personality. The disciplined, scientific, rational side of Trank documents, with clinical interest, the very emotions that carry away the impulsive, impetuous side of Trank. Although the two sides are usually in conflict, they are about evenly balanced, such that neither one dominates in the long run – and sometimes they even find themselves cooperating with each other. Here, Rational Trank calculates Impetuous Trank's chances with Miss Derring. The result is that Trank recognizes that she likes him, but not quite in that way.

Miss Derring swivels away in her chair, leaving him to use her telephone. He catches a quick glimpse of her delicate thigh, sheathed in a smooth silky stocking, as she adjusts her skirt. He makes the phone call. Tomorrow morning won't work, says Mr. Hablützel. Mr. Biland is always a top priority for him, he says, but tomorrow morning he will be in court, and there's simply nothing he can do about it. The following morning at ten would work for him. Trank lamely replies that he does not know about Mr. Biland's schedule; he needs to consult with him in this regard, and will call back later.

On the way back to the meeting room, he feels ashamed of himself for actually using such a stiff business expression as "consult with him in this regard". And he feels angry at the chairman for having him carry out these sorts of tasks.

But in truth, what does he really have to complain about? He works for a venerable institution whose prestige rubs off on him. He earns a decent salary and lives rather comfortably, though admittedly not quite luxuriously, in possession of his own home and the Saab 900 Turbo.

The house, though, is tiny – no larger than an average apartment – and sits on a tiny plot of land, which ends just a few steps from the walls of the house. And he had actually bought the Saab used, not new.

Still, back when he had been working for Professor Wickler, he could only afford to live in a mildewy three-room apartment and drive a pocket-sized Citroën. So he has made progress in his personal life, which more or less outweighs his dubious work life as a second secretary.

Or does it?

Trank feels uneasy when he tries calculating such things. "These calculations are as frustrating as the very things I'm trying to calculate," he thinks. "Enough with this."

* * *

Hartmann is now sharing his opinion on the compendium of Swiss military leaders. He tentatively declares that he could go along with having the book printed on glossy paper. As a devoted trade union secretary, he respects Switzerland's history, in which the nation's military has undoubtedly been extremely important. But it is not only the military that has been important, says Hartmann. He then casually puts forth a proposal for a book addressing the lot of the nation's lower classes – a lot which has continuously improved over the course of the preceding centuries, comprising an accomplishment that Switzerland should certainly flaunt. And by the way, he mentions, the two narratives are inextricably intertwined, as the military leaders typically would have recruited from the lower classes.

Trank yawns. It is a shame that the view from the windows is so high up. From his seat he can only see the top of the wooded hill that rises above the city, a blurry greenish silhouette in the morning haze, dotted with strange radio antennas that almost seem like bizarre works of modern art. Two high-rise buildings are also visible; the glass façade of one of them is being cleaned. He watches as the window-cleaners exercise their skillful efficient strokes, floor by floor, descending slowly until their suspended platform disappears below the lower edge of his field of vision.

Von Warteck interjects. "What, exactly, is the great historical achievement of these lower classes? Did they draft the Constitution? Establish flourishing commercial enterprises? Develop the railroad system?"

Trank, as a historian, could easily answer him, but realizes it would be pointless. Hartmann seems to realize this as well. "I apologize, I simply wanted to save time by consolidating two related agenda items," he murmurs. After the meeting he will undoubtedly latch on to Trank, attempting to start a discussion about class conflict. "What do you think about all this, as a historian?" he will ask. Trank must make sure to avoid him.

Chairman Biland turns towards Hartmann and pointedly notes that he himself has personally set the order of the items on the agenda, and that the structuring of the meeting is a matter for the one who presides over it. "Of course," Hartmann quickly replies. "There certainly is no need to change anything on my behalf."

* * *

In these kinds of situations, Trank feels sorry for Hartmann. Hartmann reminds him of his own helpless father, a patternmaker in a machine factory who immersed himself completely in his work. He shunned all other responsibilities in life, leaving Trank's mother to cope with everything.

In that regard, there was not much that Trank could learn from him. But with regard to the meticulous attention to detail required in his father's highly technical profession, Trank, when he recalls his long-dead father, likes to believe that he carried on that legacy in his own methodical scholarly work as a historian.

His pity for Hartmann disappears as soon as he has any personal interaction with him. Only within the context of the foundation's board does Hartmann come across as restrained. Alone with Trank, a dominating personality emerges.

After Trank's third meeting, Hartmann had approached him and invited him for a beer – in such a conspiratorial and discreet manner that it caught everyone's eye. Brockstätte still occasionally teases him about it.

Trank had not felt the slightest desire to have a beer with Hartmann, but he didn't have the guts to decline the offer. Regardless of whether he is prepared to face the consequences, Trank can never say no to an invitation extended to him, nor to a request for a favor. Conformity and acquiescence personified, he knows this yet is unable to change it.

Only very rarely is he capable of overcoming this submissiveness. When he gets angry, he manages to hurl trenchant, piercing words like freshly-sharpened spears, without regard for his already fragile relationships with their targets.

Fortunately, such outbursts are rare. And the satisfaction is only momentary anyhow; he always feels uncomfortable afterwards. So he either stays mellow, in which case everyone else has complete control over him, or he lets loose, in which case, strictly speaking, even he does not have control over his own self. It never balances out.

He chalks all of this up to his dichotomous personality. When he stays mellow, Rational Trank communicates using logical, well-founded arguments – and, lacking any urgent matters to attend to, he had no logical argument against going for a beer with Hartmann. But when he lets loose, on the other hand, then Impetuous Trank wreaks havoc.

Trank sighs audibly. Kindlimann shoots him a look that says, "Would you kindly spare us your girlish whimpering?"

The aftermath of the incident with Hartmann: The man spent three interminable hours, over a single beer, telling Trank all about of the board's supposed machinations against him as a union representative who works for the workers.

"They think that fool Hartmann doesn't realize. They're wrong, I'm watching everything! Even when I seem to be poring over my files. When you see von Warteck nudge Kindlimann and whisper something to him, and then Kindlimann laughs, it's almost certainly a joke at my expense. And you see how the chairman always urges me to make it brief whenever I'm talking. And isn't it obvious that Brockstätte doesn't show me the same respect that he shows the other members of the board?"

Trank doesn't agree with the conspiracy theory, but doesn't venture to interject. Hartmann is not the only one on the board to experience being favored or disfavored. For example, the chairman holds Oederlein in especially high regard, but treats Berglass quite contemptuously. Oederlein himself is close with von Warteck, while he avoids both Berglass and Kindlimann. Von Warteck admires Kindlimann, and also unsuccessfully attempts to win the chairman's favor.

That afternoon, it became clear to Trank what really afflicted Hartmann: it was that the board members treated him with a certain cruel indifference. He was not one of their group, and so he was truly of no significance to them whatsoever.

* * *

Miss Derring strides purposefully into the room. She brings Brockstätte a note, which the latter hands over to the chairman, and then she slinks away. Trank catches a glimpse of her shapely legs once again. The elegant slit of her short, tight skirt reveals the tantalizing features of her feminine thigh as she walks.

How is it that no women sit on the foundation's board despite the fact that the foundation exists just as much for their benefit as for the men's?

The men gather here, banishing women from their sight; they ruffle their own feathers and talk in platitudes. They would certainly handle the meetings quite differently, though, if just a couple of attractive women were present. They would eliminate their hours of inane, frivolous deliberations, or else lose their right to claim that men get things done more efficiently – nowadays women often tackle debates quite skillfully and ruthlessly.

And the men would definitely not continue to let themselves go in the ways they do now. Von Warteck would no longer lean back in his chair unabashedly scratching his crotch, as if to let everyone know that crabs affect even men of his high social standing. Kindlimann would finally have to do something about his nasty bad breath. And Professor Berglass would be well-advised to refrain from delivering his scathing commentaries regarding female drivers.

On the other hand, there would be even more posturing by the men, even more attempts to impress and to assert dominance. Kindlimann would dwell on the fact that he and his troops protected the country from all sorts of aggressors for so many years; Oederlein on his role as a politician in fostering the nation's growth; von Warteck on the risks he takes to provide the insurance that undergirds that very growth; and Professor Berglass on the fact that all such accomplishments would be impossible without the tireless work of the academic elite, such as himself, in cultivating a robust education system. Only Biland and Hartmann tend to eschew such displays of posturing – Biland because he stands above all of them anyway, and Hartmann because the values that he represents would simply not be appreciated here.

"Well, there you go," Trank concludes. "No matter how I spin it, these guys just are not prepared to have a woman here."

* * *

And he gives up on Miss Derring. His experience with Elisabeth has taught him that the conquest itself is more exciting than everything that happens afterwards. Only in their first embrace did he triumphantly feel, "This is it! This is just what I've been craving!" Surprisingly, though, what subsequently developed between them almost resembled a stagnant, uncomfortable marriage.

Elisabeth had a stunningly gorgeous body, yet he never even had chances to savor it. She shunned the languid explorations of his mouth and fingers, instead demanding that he take her like a wild beast. Afterward, she lay in his arms and talked, monotonously and interminably. She talked about the office, about fashion, about women's problems, even about politics – she watched the news every day, and faithfully recounted every tidbit she heard. It put Trank to sleep, and when he awoke after a brief snooze, Elisabeth was silent beside him, beautifully reproachful.

He used to stop by her apartment on the way home from work. He would arrive home not much later than usual, and it was quite believable when he blamed the delay on the traffic leaving the city. But one day, while driving home after a summer rain shower, with fresh air blowing through the car's open windows and a poignant French love song playing on the radio, he was seized by a powerful feeling. He suddenly came to the brutally honest realization that Elisabeth, despite her amazing body, simply bored him, and that she could never come close to measuring up to Maria. In that instant he understood that he had been searching for something in Elisabeth – he wasn't sure exactly what though – and that he had not found it.

So he started speculating about how he might break things off with his "insignificant other". Fortunately for him, things worked themselves out. Elisabeth met a nice guy who was either not yet married or was already divorced. "He's always there for me, even at night and on the weekends, you know," she explained, understandably jubilant. The affair ended by mutual consent.

In the weeks that followed, Trank felt a certain void in his life. Something was missing, some sort of stimulus. Anything to counter the bleakness of existence. Maybe just a small space in life for personal exploration.

Because he never occupies his time with existential issues. He operates according to a plan, a set program. Not quite like a robot, no. But rather than actively living his life, it seems his life is just passively lived. He is ensconced like a frightened animal in a thicket of obligations, demands, expectations.

Opportunities for change are few and far between. They require risks to be taken. Steps into the unknown.

* * *

Professor Berglass is a man who tends to get swept up in the moment. "Gentlemen," he says, "an idea has just come to me: for the seven-hundred-year anniversary, why don't we commission a book on the history of the country's two smallest minorities, the Jews and the gypsies?"

"Then we can go one step further and celebrate the homosexuals and the drug addicts!" Oederlein snaps. Before the discussion can get out of hand, Chairman Biland raps on the table with his silver pen and says, "Please put forth your proposals now; I want each of them to be voted upon." Trank counts the raised hands, announces the results, and records them in the minutes.

It is now settled: The foundation has unanimously decided to furnish a grant for the financing of the book on Swiss military leaders. And for this book only.

2

Gerold Trank's river of thoughts has fiercely swept him away in its treacherous current this morning, as if he were a spongy piece of driftwood; it seems certain to ultimately send him plummeting down a long, thunderous waterfall. Without a doubt, it would be in Trank's best interests to swim vigorously right now toward the solid ground on its banks, to save himself while he still has a chance.

His body is bound with invisible shackles to his chrome-plated, burgundy-upholstered chair, which in turn is tightly fused to the dove grey carpeting on the floor. Yet still, his spirit continues to float about freely. Nothing that is said here can pin it down, restrain it. The disintegrating ropes of life's daily pressures can no longer tether it in place. Trank's spirit retreats into the depths of its host, sinking down to the bottom where it can build itself up once again.

Now he wants to get to the root of things. For once not in an aloof theoretical manner, but using the actual practical example of Gerold Trank, second secretary at FPHI, failed historian, failed lover, and barely adequate family man.

And this time he will do it without pathetic excuses. Burdened by disappointment over his failings and driven by a strange sort of hunger, he will likely once again assume the grim facial expressions of his cramped youth. These expressions always used to upset his poor mother. "Life is so short," she would say, "let's at least be happy."

One thing is clear: for years he has simply drifted, without bothering to ask who exactly he is, what exactly he is doing, or what exactly he wants to accomplish in his limited lifespan. Eight years, thrown away – just like that.

If Trank doesn't think about his own life, then it is only others who will think about it for him. Nowadays, everyone has opinions about what he should do as an employee, as a citizen, as a consumer of the media. Opinions that are sometimes whispered into his ear, and sometimes hammered into his skull.

Whatever plan he develops must manage to get him out of his rut. First, though, he must cleanse his mind, get it to start functioning soundly once again. The bugs that have somehow snuck into its operating system must be fixed. Otherwise, he will inevitably set out on the wrong path.

"Come on, start thinking ahead!" urges Impetuous Trank. "That's your job! I just pull the trigger."

Alright, time to think rationally now.

According to its bylaws, FPHI fosters humanism. That would all be well and good, if it were only true. Trank sees nothing at the foundation, though, that advances humanism – unless "humanism" is taken to mean "socializing in exclusive Swiss clubs". For him, though, there is none of that. Instead, he spends all his time working on trivial projects – projects in which he sees nothing valuable or exciting, projects from which no existential need will be met. Everything is for show. It doesn't make any difference to him whether these projects are implemented or not.

But if he is not serving the cause, then whom exactly is he serving?

People, of course. People who have managed to climb to a higher social status and to successfully make themselves matter. They evaluate what he can offer them, and then they use him as they wish. More precisely, they use him to their own advantage. Although, as a historian, he is familiar with Machiavelli's writings, Trank has never actually thought of himself in this manner. "I walk around like I've got a cloak of invisibility," he thinks, "but in reality I'm fully visible, naked and exposed."

"We haven't been paying attention, and we're suffering as a result," Impetuous Trank hisses through clenched teeth. "We can't put up with this any longer, we have to resist!"

"But there's an even simpler option that we also need to consider," replies Rational Trank. "I can recognize that my circumstances are shaped by forces beyond my control, and that they were thus inevitable. Then I can finally come to terms with everything and accept it."

"No, impossible!" exclaims Impetuous Trank. "You can't just resign yourself like that without putting up a fight. You've been in turmoil ever since that encounter with Maria's brother that set everything in motion."

"It's absolutely not impossible," Rational Trank counters. "It simply depends upon me finding a plausible explanation. Don't forget, I specialized in the medieval period, an entire millennium during which every individual's status at birth immutably determined his status for the rest of his life. So if I can only identify some underlying historical principle that fits, then I would be able to calm down and finally just lead a relaxed, comfortable life. I would have my place in the social structure, and not a bad one at that: a secretary at a highly prestigious institution whose luster reflects well upon myself by extension – just look at that glossy promotional brochure that Brockstätte is gloating about at this very moment."

Impetuous Trank says nothing.

"If I could just come to terms with it," Rational

Trank argues further, "then I would have a very different outlook on life, always experiencing the moment, never worrying about long-term perspectives. I could just enjoy the moment – or curse the moment, as the case may be – and, recognizing that all existential rancor is futile, blithely carry on with the rest of my life."

Impetuous Trank still says nothing.

Trank observes that there is really only one set of circumstances in which he fully savors the moment. It happens in the evenings, when he lies on the couch in his living room, his headphones disconnecting him completely from the world, listening to one of his highbrow jazz albums, like Keith Jarrett's Arbour Zena or McCoy Tyner's Sahara. This music is not tied to any physical space, only to time itself. He feels like he is floating. Like the world is his oyster.

* * *

Meanwhile, Oederlein has begun inundating the room with his parliamentary eloquence. "Switzerland must avoid isolation and learn to orient itself within Europe," he affirms. "But that does not mean capitulating to Brussels and agreeing to terms whose only purpose is to rob us of our precious individuality. If we do so, we end up sidelined even further. It is absolutely crucial for us to put great emphasis on that which is uniquely Swiss, and to bring Europe closer to our own fundamentally democratic way of thinking."

"What precious individuality is he talking about?" Trank asks himself. "We really are not so different from other people. When Oederlein rattles off these lines, it's all about keeping people like me disconnected from the rest of the world, keeping our simple little country sheltered."

Oederlein's comments are in reference to the foundation's new brochure, which has been designed by a pricey advertising agency. The agency representatives have insisted to Biland and Brockstätte that their communications to the public must contain conspicuous references to the broader Europe.

Oederlein leans back, puts his fingertips together, and continues his discourse. "And another thing," he says, "the foundation is not a government body, thank god, but rather a sort of public institution. As a member of the National Council, I always do my utmost to ensure that government brochures are not printed on glossy paper. Such printing costs must be kept to a minimum when tax money is being spent; it is the contents that must be persuasive. And the foundation should also act accordingly."

Kindlimann applauds.

"I agree with Mr. Oederlein, of course," Brockstätte interjects. "The second secretary was responsible for choosing the paper."

Everyone looks at Trank questioningly. "The price quotes for glossy paper were no more expensive than the price quotes for normal paper," he tentatively explains, "I myself was quite surprised by this."

Brockstätte brushes him off. "It can still be changed, right? No, let me correct myself, this absolutely must be changed – I just now realized that we must avoid even sending the impression that we are wasting money."

Von Warteck raises his hand with a smile on his face. "The General Life Insurance Company is also a sort of public institution, but we still print our brochures on glossy paper. Research has actually shown that the intended audience would otherwise have doubts about the company's financial stability. And incidentally, let me make one more remark: There are photos of the board members in the brochure, but not of the first secretary, and I think this is wrong. We don't actually need to show the entire staff, of course; that would be going too far. But the first secretary is basically one of us."

His colleagues on the board express their approval. Hartmann sits up and opens his mouth to say something, but then sinks back down silently. Brockstätte, meanwhile, looks around with a modest smile on his face.

* * *

Impetuous Trank seethes. Meanwhile Rational Trank, completely indifferent to the question of whether his picture appears in the brochure, contemplates an unsettling question: Is there some underlying law that gives certain people their power?

Take Chairman Biland. Slender and elegant, with a healthy, angular face and well-coiffed grey hair. He is a business school graduate and was the general manager of a major bank before he took over the foundation. Some career-minded friends whom Trank regularly meets for lunch say, "Biland is a great example of how anyone can rise up to a high position in our country."

But was it his background that had gently propelled him ahead in life?

When Trank's mother drops by for a Sunday lunch, she always asks her son what he did at work last week. Trank hates discussing this topic, but he crafts a polite answer for her: he wrote up the minutes of meetings, he drafted letters, he did all the things that secretaries do. His mother nods. "Of course you have to do what the others tell you to do," she sometimes says, "but it's nice that you've gotten quite far considering your background."

Trank gets the uneasy feeling that this is actually some kind of knock on him. But then he thinks of some of his former classmates from influential upper-class families who are now down-and-out, worthless good-for-nothings. Life just passes them by. Meanwhile, they philosophize despondently about how the world is messed up, all the time just digging themselves deeper into their holes. So, it seems that he can definitely eliminate one's background as the underlying determining principle, as the fundamental prescript that determines one's destiny.

One's own capabilities are more important, in fact. "Skilled people are always in demand," his father used to say, with regard to himself. The machine factory where he worked was always booming, and he spent fifty years there. He had first done an apprenticeship there, and was then hired even before he was old enough for conscription into the army. Trank recalls one summer afternoon while he was still a student, during which he explained to his father the Chinese Mandarin system of appointing officials based on results from imperial examinations, a system that was created in order to ensure that the most capable people were always put in charge of running the empire.

But is it really always the most skilled who come out ahead? What about all of the geniuses who go unnoticed during their lifetimes, before being "discovered" posthumously? As a historian, he is well aware of the fact that skills and capabilities alone are not enough. They do play a role, but are no more determinative or decisive than one's background.

So, what else is there?

Personal ambition. What one wants to achieve in life. Each individual following his or her own inner compass.

Trank is a bundle of inhibitions, and the needle of his inner compass does not stop wobbling, constantly changing direction. In Brockstätte's compass, it points unwaveringly upward. Although younger, he ranks above Trank at the foundation; Elisabeth had often brought this fact to Trank's attention.

During a recent coffee break, the female secretaries at the foundation, always up-to-date on the latest gossip, dished that Brockstätte wanted to be chairman of the foundation himself one day. "Why not?" said the caretaker from his smoking corner. "He just authorized a new carpet-cleaning machine, so he's got my vote."

"Because it's an unwritten rule of the game," Trank replied. "One can only become chairman after reaching the pinnacle of one's career in either business or government or the military."

"And you really believe that baloney?" the caretaker laughed. "Every kid knows you can change the rules of the game when you need to."

And, in a certain sense, Brockstätte has already reached the board members' level. He discusses parliamentary matters with Oederlein. He is regularly invited to spend the weekend at von Warteck's vacation cottage, a converted sheep barn in Graubünden. And he has done military service under Kindlimann, often joining in the ex-general's famous drinking sessions.

Brockstätte's conviction that his personal goals are achievable, as well as his assertiveness in driving himself towards their achievement, raises him above Trank's level. Trank never even thought of setting such goals for himself. He believes that noble men demand nothing for themselves, such as doctors and lawyers who volunteer their services for the needy. Rather, they strive and live for the good of the community. It is a dogma to which he was exposed long ago, which makes him believe that those who act otherwise evince a dishonorable mentality.

But is it really so? No, it is nonsense. The only ones who need such principles are weak people who lack direction; Trank certainly has always been such a person.

He feels some answers beginning to crystallize within his cascade of thoughts.

"He who cannot command himself, remains forever a slave." Who had said this? Probably Goethe. Definitely Goethe. Trank had written an essay about it for his university entrance exam; he hasn't thought about it for twenty years.

Back when he worked as Professor Wickler's assistant, he had jokingly nicknamed himself " Servus Wicklerius". But it was a serious situation, not a laughing matter. And now he was ashamed of how he always tended to either joke about such unpleasant situations or else simply sugarcoat them, instead of actually doing something to resolve them.

And this is the case with regard to his current situation as well. Chairman Biland personally attends to the interests of National Council member Oederlein. Brockstätte looks after Kindlimann and von Warteck. After Biland took the cherry from the top of the cake, and Brockstätte licked off the frosting, Trank was stuck with the doughy remnants – Berglass and Hartmann.

And how did he respond to this situation? Well, at first he tried to appeal to Berglass as a fellow academic. But Berglass is a professor of architecture, not history; the two fields intersect only in the deserted realm of art history, and Berglass now uses their mutual fondness for medieval cathedrals to bother Trank about his projects, always trying to get Trank to reveal the easiest ways to get at the foundation's funds.

And with regard to Hartmann, Trank convinced himself that connecting with such a representative of the people was even more valuable than connecting with the big shots – with the result that Hartmann ended up conducting himself like an even bigger shot whenever dealing with Trank.

All these ruminations are clearing things up a bit for Trank. He now recognizes his problem: he doesn't know what he wants.

So, is he destined to continue in this manner forever? Or can he, too, set a goal for himself, and wrench himself free from the clutches of those who order him around?

Why is he suddenly seeing everything so clearly this morning? What has made these meaningful insights come to him now, while sitting in this boring meeting? How is Rational Trank now analyzing the situation so coolly, while Impetuous Trank sits there gnashing his teeth?

For weeks, Trank has not been sleeping well. He wakes up tossing and turning in the middle of the night, the bed creaking annoyingly beneath him. His feels a stifling heat, despite the coldish temperatures. Thoughts swirl around inside his head. Thoughts of which he can make no sense. Fortunately, Maria is fast asleep while all this happens.

Sometimes he is beset by nocturnal cramps for no apparent reason. Stiffness in his neck, twinges in his chest. His jaw is clenched.

Then, he peels the warm bedding off his body, gets out of bed, and does something unusual. He mixes some warm milk and whiskey and stands in his pajamas at the kitchen window for at least half an hour, looking out into the bluish night, at the neatly trimmed bushes and the bare concrete walls and the perfectly paved road – a sad landscape with no horizon, a view that does nothing to relax him. Or he sneaks into the kitchen with a sort of indefinable hunger, a feeling that he simply needs to ingest something. Down his throat he forces a block of Tilsit cheese that does not agree with him; half an hour later he vomits the cheese back out into the toilet. It is no longer identifiable as cheese. He is so disgusted that, when Maria asks him in the morning, he acknowledges only having eaten the cheese, nothing more.

So it appears that some unknown mechanism had already been set in motion inside him, and thus he now finds himself engaged in deep introspection this morning. This is something new for him. On one hand it's embarrassing, as it feels wrong (narcissistic weakness and all that); but on the other hand it's exciting, as it will end up making things easier for him.

What is the use of this soul-searching anyway? Mostly it's a catharsis. A purgatory, on his path to redemption. Trank constantly finds himself using these terms even though he abandoned religion long ago, while he was still a student. And why is this catharsis necessary? Because, in the last eight years, Trank's soul simply has not gotten much release.

He hasn't had a chance to just spread his thoughts right out before himself, like he had once done along the rocky beach on Belle-Île. There, all his anxiety just dispersed into the blue horizon.

He has occupied himself with nothing but petty, everyday concerns. His daily life is hectic, with thousands of small problems perpetually besieging him. All entirely insignificant, yet still nerve-wracking.

His superiors are obsessed with frenetic activity. They relentlessly concoct new endeavors, most of which Trank finds ephemeral and absolutely unnecessary. Yet he has no choice but to carry out their plans.

* * *

The board is now addressing the budget. All items will be adjusted to account for inflation. Is that all? Not yet.

The caretaker will get a bonus; skilled workers are always in high demand. And Brockstätte requests an additional secretary; both the number of applications to be processed and the amount of funds to be managed are on the increase.

"That's all true," Professor Berglass protests, "but with Mr. Chairman's secretary and Mr. Brockstätte's secretary and Trank's part-timer, and a bookkeeper as well, you already have an exorbitant amount of support staff in comparison with how it is at the university."

"Professor, you're comparing apples and oranges once again," Oederlein snaps back. "I second the motion, it's more than justified. Period."

Von Warteck chimes in as well. "Comparing the size of the foundation's staff with the amount of funds it is dealing with, this extra secretary seems necessary. Of course we would have to take a closer look at the situation, but I believe we can trust in Mr. Brockstätte's operational experience."

* * *

"The operations are expanding," thinks Trank, as he is beset by a pessimistic vision. "Retired at sixty-five, I look back on my decades of working life, in which, isolated from what happens in the real world, I have done absolutely nothing meaningful. Even if I had not done any of what I did, it would have made no real difference anyway. My entire professional life was just for show – and not only that, it was all in accordance with what others ordered me to do."

"What do you mean, 'isolated from what happens in the real world'?" asks Impetuous Trank.

"Everything that is linked to existence," replies Rational Trank, after a brief hesitation. "Tangible suffering, hunger, anguish, murder in all its forms, sickness, love, emergency help, anything that gives meaning to existence, the fulfillment of needs, the realization of possibilities. Why should all these things play out only in my private life, while my work life remains isolated and sterile?"

"Wait a second," says Impetuous Trank, "our private life is just as sterile. You must admit, it's dominated by petty obligations in exactly the same way. Just look at all the things that you have to deal with as the man of the house: hammering in nails, lugging boxes around, fixing bicycles and all that, then picking up Maria's elderly parents or our own frail mother from the railway station while Maria prepares Sunday lunch because the ten-minute walk is just too much for them already. And then after dinner each day, even when there's nothing physical that needs to get done, there are all those little conversations with Maria and the kids, those little conversations that are necessary when you're raising a family."

"And Maria's day-to-day life is no different," Trank realizes. "But still, she tells me that if I took on less work, then I wouldn't be coming home so exhausted every day. That certainly sounds reasonable, but it's far from being a reality, because it's impossible for me to accomplish that without first taking a step back from what I'm doing. And since I lack any sort of broad perspective, I thus also lack any sort of tranquility."

Only a great visionary task, against which all others pale in comparison, would suffice to restore Trank's perspective, to bring him closer to "what happens in the real world". His perspective of the passage of time, in particular, has disappeared; his energies are wholly concentrated on the task at hand at any particular instant.

He has completely lost his sense of time – despite the fact that he is an historian, who lives and breathes timelines. Trank would like to be able to survey the entire timespan of his life, from birth to death, to give himself a benchmark for assessment of any particular moment along the way.

* * *

While Major General Kindlimann rhapsodizes about the old Confederation, laments the lack of military preparedness among Swiss citizens nowadays, and urges that intense efforts be made during the 700th anniversary year to combat this serious crisis, Trank is realizing that all of his hustling and bustling is meaningless if it doesn't lead to anything. He should constantly be thinking about his life as if in retrospect, from the moment of his own death. He realizes that if he were to die today, his obituary would likely contain no indication of how he had actually spent his life.

He thinks of Maria's nephew Alex, who was quite humbly making his way through life as a musician, and who has recently gifted him an album on which he performed.

And what could Trank possibly give to Alex in return? At best one of the foundation's quarterly reports that he has painstakingly compiled, a masterpiece of bureaucratic work – though written solely for the archives. And, of course, entirely determined by circumstances over which Trank has no control.

What about a radical solution? Like just running away? Over the course of the last few weeks he has pondered various escape possibilities, but never thought them through to their conclusions. Visualizing such a plan all the way through to its end is stressful and requires courage. Images of the future become increasingly blurrier. And there's a growing fear of finding no solution, of the situation following him wherever he goes.

Trank wants to solve the problem now. And if he can determine that running away is not a solution, then that will help him. He decides to think through one escape scenario of which he is particularly fond – all the way to its end.

He will stop at the used car dealer on his way into the city in the morning (the one right at the city limits with the flashy signs that scream "Cash now for your old car!!!"), and offer to sell the Saab. It works. So says Maria's brother (Alex's father, in fact), an independent civil engineer, who once urgently needed money to close a deal after maxing out his credit line.

He will need to demonstrate that he is the rightful owner of the car, and will ask for about fifteen thousand francs. "Twelve thousand, cash in hand!" the dealer will reply, with a cocky grin and an exuberant slap on Trank's shoulder.

With twelve thousand, he could disappear abroad. But where?

Brittany? No, too sentimental and too obvious.

Germany? Austria? No way, their citizens are just as mistrustful and xenophobic as the Swiss. They would smell something fishy and immediately report it to the police.

Italy appeals to him, especially Tuscany. But no, there are standing plans to drive there in two weeks with Maria and the children – the summer holidays are just around the corner.

The best option, it seems to him, is the Iberian peninsula, with its aloof, confident, and courteous population.

One hour later he has booked a Swissair flight to Lisbon. Seven hours from now, Maria will realize he is gone. Breaking away from his past life is an awful process, but he must think ruthlessly now. The problem of preserving his ties to the family, which he cannot repudiate no matter how strong his desire to escape, will have to be solved later. "My mistake," he tells himself, "is that in these situations I always think first of my family. It's like they are fibers of a cocoon that still envelops me."

The stewardess smiles at him, and shows him where to stow his carry-on luggage. It is a light canvas bag with a silly promotional imprint, containing a toothbrush, a shaving kit, a washcloth, pajamas, underwear, two shirts, and a light sweater that he bought in the airport.

After arriving in Lisbon to pleasant, breezy weather, he finds a cheap guesthouse in the old part of town. He takes in the musty air, the tangy smells, the clatter of workshops, the unintelligible bits of conversation, and the fado music that is coming from somewhere. He spends his time looking around for work. Wait, that's far too naïve of him. In Lisbon, his Ph.D. in history and his experience as a secretary will get him nowhere. He has neither the language skills necessary to work as a tour guide nor the muscles necessary to work in construction or at the docks.

If he could only play a musical instrument like Alex. And Alex is accustomed to bare subsistence living anyway; he could definitely manage to survive here. Trank, inspired by the jazz albums that he loves, had always wanted to learn how to play the saxophone. Well, maybe Lisbon was just not the right destination?

* * *

Trank's train of thought is interrupted.

Miss Derring has entered the room once again; she traipses over to the chairman with her long, shapely legs, and she leans over the table to place a signature folder in front of him. She is wearing a low-cut summer blouse, and Trank, sitting directly opposite the chairman, gets a nice glimpse of her cleavage. It is a favor that destiny has already bestowed upon him a couple of times before. Miss Derring's is the sort of cleavage that manifests promise of even greater things, and he finds himself vividly imagining her naked breasts on her perfect naked body.

Impetuous Trank revels in this, but Rational Trank rebukes him. "Why even bother? Just remember the little 'adventure' with Elisabeth."

Even Rational Trank admits, though, that sex is just a part of life; in fact, it is the entire basis for life itself. Sexual thoughts can only be suppressed by force, only with spiritual retreat, with meditation, with a general process of decarnalization.

* * *

Back in Lisbon, he is facing the same problem. He must inevitably encounter a woman there. In line with the many literary precedents, she would likely be quite pretty and younger than Trank. Maybe a prostitute.

That could actually be convenient, as there is really only a certain kind of woman who would enter the picture here. A young, hardened woman, who would not immediately start investigating his background and his income, but who has rather learned not to ask questions, and who accepts him as she sees him: as an interesting middle-aged foreign man of average build, with a gaunt, not unattractive face, and, at the moment, nine thousand francs in his newly-opened bank account.

If necessary, he will pass himself off as a civil engineer. He has spent many interminable summer afternoons listening to Maria's brother drone on about his work; maybe all that sacrifice will not have been in vain. And, in his day-to-day life, the chances are very low that he will actually bump into someone who is a professional in the field.

Trank soon settles into his new life. It goes without saying that he moves in with his new girlfriend. The apartment is in a decent building in the Chiado neighborhood, far enough away from the sleazy hotel near Avenida da Liberdade where she works.

He spends the first few relaxed weeks going for long walks, visiting the art exhibitions at the Gulbenkian Museum, and reading. Fortunately, Portugal has long maintained close ties with England, and he finds many bookshops and kiosks at Rossio Square that are stocked with English books. He enjoys doing nothing – or to put it more elegantly, being free.

His girlfriend plies her trade, goes shopping, cooks for him, and washes his underwear. Once she has grown close enough to Trank to start envisioning a long-term future with him, she will give up her trade (one that was considered dishonorable even in medieval times, but whatever), and seek a more "bourgeois" career. As a shopgirl in one of the large new malls on the outskirts of the city, or maybe in a classy shop in the Pombaline Lower Town. (And no, Professor Berglass, she won't be one of those shopgirls with a car to clog up the streets!) It leaves Trank free to manage the household and study Portuguese.

Wait a second. There it is again! He is automatically thinking of himself in a responsible role within the solid framework of a bourgeois existence. But why? Because he simply does not have his own life plan. And that's exactly the point here.

In this daydream, why does he not see himself as a man with no obligations or responsibilities, as a man who lets his girl keep turning tricks while he wastes his days in Lisbon's pool halls and beats her when she doesn't obey him?

He always concerns himself with those around him and with their expectations of him. This can definitely be considered a personality flaw. He never takes care of his own interests. His foolish heart is always beating for others. He constantly feels like he has to solve everyone else's problems whenever those problems have come about through any sort of connection to himself.

Even when Maria's brother recently suggested that he find a new job. Instead of thinking first of his own interests, he instantly thought about the difficulties that Brockstätte would face in trying to fill the vacancy left by his unexpected departure.

"This is exactly how I have been alienating me from my own self," Rational Trank observes.

"This is infuriating!" says Impetuous Trank, "I need to stop acting like this. I need to bust out, to make some kind of brand new start."

"It's no use," says Rational Trank. "This is just how I am. It would take lots of time to change me."

"Right, that's just how we are. Look, we even built that nesting box above our bedroom balcony for the redstarts that appeared on our block last May, and then the damn things annoyed us all summer long with their constant chirping. And they mucked up the whole balcony too."

Fortunately, Trank is now in Lisbon, far from those damn birds. He is here because adventure really is possible. Because one can will it to happen, just as soon as one's qualms and inhibitions are overcome – if one only has the courage to realize his dreams.

Of course, however, a person first must be able to dream. He must dream his way out of the insipid atmosphere of everyday life. Everyday life, adventure – two things that have always been mutually incompatible, as far as Trank was concerned.

People watch movies to pretend that they are living out adventures. They feel a temporary need for something exciting – a harmless little war, maybe a quick revolution. Unfortunately, it doesn't always go the way they want, and they soon find themselves fed up with the mud and blood of the trenches; then, they simply return to their boring lives.

Incidentally, his own little "adventure" with Elisabeth definitely did not quite live up to his original expectations either.

So he'll have to be careful. His adventure in Lisbon may also go wrong – and the possible negative outcomes suddenly seem more likely than the potential rosy outcomes.

For instance: Perhaps he befriends other loafers like himself in the dimly-lit pool hall that he frequents. Shady characters, but (as far as he can tell with his limited language skills) they treat him with extreme courtesy. The only thing he finds strange is that his prostitute girlfriend actually disapproves of them. Ultimately, though, in this new phase of his life, he just doesn't care enough to do anything but ignore her.

One evening, his money runs out. He simply can't match up with the expert pool players here, and he should have stopped playing long ago. But he could not stop. When he tries to leave, they laugh and give him a friendly slap on the back; they tell him it's no fun playing without him, and they order him another glass of port.

The last game has been lost, and he cannot pay what he owes. The atmosphere immediately becomes tense; his cohorts suddenly seem threatening. The congenial attitude has disappeared completely. He empties his pockets – not a cent. They rip off his jacket and violently haul him to the door. The employees and the other guests are watching, but act as if they see nothing. One of his supposed "friends" gruffly warns him never to set foot in the establishment again.

Trank is out on the street with no money and no papers. And it abruptly dawns on him that he is desperate. He had burned through his own money long ago – and he has been living off his girlfriend's earnings since then. She becomes like an angel in his eyes. His only hope.

He sets off to look for her at the sleazy hotel where she earns her living. She is neither there nor in the surrounding alleyways. It is a bleak, cold January night, and a loathsome rain has begun to fall. He heads for their shared apartment in the Chiado.

The windows of the apartment are dark, the building door is locked, and his key is still in the jacket that was ripped off of him at the pool hall. He loiters around the building entrance, and realizes that he is arousing suspicion. The few passersby stare at him, seeing a desperate-looking man with no jacket and wet clothes.

He heads for the Rossio railway station, in order to warm up a bit. He wants to make a phone call, but he would need to beg for the money – and he does not have the nerve to do so. A police officer starts taking notice of him. He decides to leave.

Back to the Chiado. The light is on in the apartment. Thank god, his girlfriend is home. He continuously rings the bell, but she doesn't open the door. He steps back out into the street and tries to call up towards the windows of the apartment, but his voice does not even manage to shout; instead, he just croaks weakly. He is seriously starting to catch a cold. He is wet and wretchedly freezing. And starving. He would give anything right now for a warm soup – something he had turned down so many times in his old, comfortable life.

He begins to realize that fate has thoroughly destroyed him in a matter of a few hours. He is now nothing more than a ragged tramp on the brink of existence. He has no idea where or how he will survive this night, where or how he can find a warm, dry place. Even living like a tramp is something that he would have to learn.

And this is the moment that he surrenders.

He heads for the nearest police station. Exhausted and chilled to the bone, he is overjoyed when they let him spend the night in a warm, stinky cell. The next day he manages to convince the police officers that he is from Switzerland and that he has been robbed. And – praise fate! – they contact the embassy. After a bit of administrative back-and-forth, he is on his way back to Switzerland.

It will be a humiliating return. And he is not even

sure whether his family will accept him back, after he had simply abandoned them like that.

With this exact thought, he realizes just how much he would have missed his family. And so, it seems that playing out the full escape scenario has only demonstrated to him what he already knew: he is either too soft or too scrupled to start leading such a selfish, exploitative life.

Such an escape clearly is not the solution for him. He will not flutter about in panic like a beheaded chicken. No more daydreams then, no more contrived illusions. He must get out of his current situation some other way.

It does not suffice to know what he does not want, and to simply flee from it. He must also figure out what he actually does want, and then devise some strategy for achieving it. Just like the men on the foundation's board have done.

* * *

Trank is once again torn from his thoughts. The president puts the approval of the quarterly report to a vote, then announces a break, and asks Trank to tally the votes and to have Miss Derring bring in some coffee.

3

The door is nudged open by a shapely derriere. Miss Derring pulls a nicely arranged serving cart into the room, laden with coffeepots, mugs, sugar, and creamer. Trank automatically stands up to help her. As he reaches to take one of the gold-rimmed mugs from the cart, his hand accidentally brushes against Miss Derring's breast. Impetuous Trank wants to take advantage of this delicious and exciting event after the meeting – a gallant, well-formulated apology, crafted by Rational Trank, would be a perfect way to strike up a flirty conversation.

Rational Trank blows off the idea. "We don't have time for such games. We have to focus on our courageous look far into the future – as far ahead as we can see, to the very horizon. And we have to figure out what path will best lead us there."

While the internal debate is taking place, Trank fails to notice Brockstätte's reproachful glare. He sits back down and, as Miss Derring finally pours his own coffee, thanks her with a slight nod. "Much too brief and casual," says Impetuous Trank, "she's clearly expecting something more."

* * *

Trank has an excuse for his lack of attention; he is experiencing a mild attack of nausea. While playing out his initially-exciting-but-ultimately-failed escape to Lisbon, he has accidentally inhaled some of his cigar smoke.

Or is the nausea just due to his general fatigue? To the fact that he is just plain strung out? His nerves, protected for all these years by a thick, cottony layer of repression, are once again exposed. Over these last few sleepless weeks, a certain weariness has built up inside him and sapped his ability to loosen up; it correlates with his uncomfortable realization that his entire lifestyle is unnatural and illusory. Just look at the work he has done – look at the foundation's quarterly report, for example. Could it possibly be anything other than the work of a man with a decaying mind?

"I should do something about my health," he thinks. "Quit smoking, drink less, finally start taking the family for some hikes on the weekend."

He reflects on a newspaper clipping that he has carried around in his wallet for six months, one which he can't bring himself to throw away due to the impact that the article still has on him. In a sober and scientific manner, it explains how poor people tend to age worse than the rich, as they are more likely to have lifestyles that include unhealthy habits such as poor nutrition, smoking, and alcohol abuse; they are thus more likely to expose themselves to all of the risks that are inherent in such lifestyles. The article speculates regarding exactly why this is true. But in any case, social class is definitely a decisive factor.

Trank had felt the article was applicable to himself as well. In material terms, he could by no means be considered a poor person. But his proletarian background has never allowed him to feel otherwise.

Oederlein's own humble roots served as a driving force for his rise up the ladder; in Trank's case, though, it has only bogged him down. With a renewed sense of disgust, he vividly recalls scenes from the past in which his inhibitions and humility manifested themselves. He always struggles desperately with the problem of finding his bearings in higher social circles. And whenever he is compelled to actually speak, he always says the wrong thing.

* * *

The coffee break (or mineral water break for von Warteck, as unlike Trank he is mindful of his sensitive stomach) puts the meeting on hold for ten minutes. This time, as Brockstätte once pointed out, gives the board members an opportunity to establish closer ties with each other, maybe score some lucrative business, or simply exchange a few spicy upper-class gossip tidbits.

Von Warteck has cornered the chairman and is talking him up quite fervently. Their murmurs reach Trank's ears, but he cannot make out a single word.

Hartmann and Berglass have found themselves on the topic of minorities; they are in agreement that certain actions must be taken in favor of historically marginalized groups, especially during the upcoming anniversary year.

Brockstätte has joined Oederlein, who is explaining how he helped quash the latest parliamentary motion regarding interest rates on mortgages. Oederlein has reached the end of one of his imported cigarettes, and, without bothering to crush it, flicks the butt into one of the plant pots that line the wall of the room. Trank uncharacteristically feels nothing when he sees this; the plants are identical, uninteresting rubber plants, chosen indifferently.

Kindlimann now comes and sits next to Trank. Trank moves his chair back to avoid the ex-general's notoriously bad breath. It proves to be futile, as Kindlimann responds by moving closer. He was always too conceited to use ear protectors while in the army, so he is already going somewhat deaf. A wave of foul air hits Trank. His nausea instantly intensifies.

"Listen," says Kindlimann, "I remember you once got me some of those rubber gaskets from Ulmer & Kellenberger for my garden hose. By the way, did you know I actually served with old Kellenberger? He rose as high as brigadier in the artillery corps. He actually died a couple of years ago, even though he lived quite a healthy lifestyle. Anyway, I need another two packages of gaskets now, can I give you the measurements, and you pick them up? You pass by there every day anyway on your way into the city."

Actually, Trank doesn't pass anywhere near there, a fact that he had tried to make Kindlimann understand the last time he was asked. But Kindlimann had launched into a huge discussion of Trank's exact route to the workplace, until eventually Trank just gave in and agreed that he could stop by Ulmer & Kellenberger with only a slight detour. He picked up the gaskets and sent them to Kindlimann in one of the foundation's envelopes. He did not receive a word of thanks in return.

Earlier, Trank himself had felt that Kindlimann had the right to ask him for assistance even on personal matters that were unrelated to the foundation. Now, with a calm that surprises even himself, he proclaims, "Mr. Kindlimann, in order to help you out, I would have to make a very significant detour, and these days I simply don't have the time. But I think you can easily call and order the gaskets over the phone; they might not even charge you any shipping costs."

"Oh, I couldn't insist that you make such an effort," Kindlimann declares, turning red, "especially if you're as busy as you say. I know, everyone thinks only of himself these days." He pushes himself to his feet and says remorsefully, "I used to have tons of aides and orderlies, basically an entire division's worth of them. But nowadays I have to take care of everything myself, obviously it would be nice to get a bit of assistance." He then walks back to his seat.

Trank pictures Kindlimann going to complain to Brockstätte later on. "I only asked a tiny favor of him, really just a small errand, and he could easily have taken a big burden off my shoulders. But instead he brushed me off, just like that. I'm telling you, he's a cheeky little fellow; you'd better keep an eye on him."

* * *

Impetuous Trank congratulates Rational Trank. "Finally! You always act like the big things you do for others are nothing, mere trifles. Yet you are overcome with emotion and gratitude for even the smallest things that others do for you."

"Is it really the case," Rational Trank asks himself, "that I always tend to value my own actions less than I value the actions of others? There's no reason it should be this way. Though I suppose it's true that my parents felt that they themselves were worth less than the high society people. They always made this quite clear. It's as if all those bourgeois revolutionary movements simply went right over our heads."

The historian in Trank could easily place this within an established historical context, and he smiles indulgently. But what had escaped him was that his parents had apparently foisted their own ingrained hierarchical worldview upon him as well. As a result, for all these years, he has been developing an existence that is completely futile. And in his old age he will be stuck looking back upon a meaningless life.

Trank hears a harsh inner voice – which bears a

suspicious resemblance to the chairman's – saying, "You are, in fact, a nothing. You, like most people on this earth, are here in order to selflessly serve others. It is not up to you to decide whether what you are doing is meaningful or not. That is the job of those who actually matter. So just be content with what you have accomplished in your life."

"Nonsense!" retorts Impetuous Trank. "I just had an intriguing thought," he then says to Rational Trank. "In a sort of adaptation of Descartes' method, I can observe that my inner turmoil is evidence not only of the fact that I exist, but that something exists deep inside of me from which I am increasingly alienating myself. If I take this thought even further, then there must be something primordial that is buried deep inside me right now – and I don't mean something crude like egoism, hedonism, narcissism, certainly not reckless bravado, but rather some sort of natural tendency towards following a life path that is based exclusively upon my own propensities, capabilities, and limitations. And that is the path that I need to follow if I want to achieve inner harmony."

If he follows this path, he must feel like he is moving forward in synchronicity with the flow of time itself. Only then can he feel like he is one with the particular sequence of events that is unfolding.

Has he ever had such a feeling before?

Absolutely. It was after he had turned his back on that old windbag Wickler, leaving behind his academic career, breaking free in a cold fury after he had been forsaken. On the tranquil, wide-open stretch of Belle-Île's rocky beach, calmed by the rolling waves, his feelings had started evolving in a similar direction, before the letter from the foundation had torn him away.

And it had also happened even earlier, while he

was courting Maria. After their return from France, where their lifelines had been inextricably inter- twined, his mind was completely taken over by the no- tion of carrying their holiday fling forward into a real relationship.

He lived his entire life towards achieving this goal. He arranged everything in his life specifically in order to be able see her as often as possible.

He started working as Wickler's assistant at that time. He would head to the Institute each morning and feverishly await his lunch break, during which he picked Maria up at the bank where she was working. At first, they would eat their sandwiches together in one of the city's many parks; later, when the weather got colder, they started frequenting the cheapest res- taurants they could find.

They would meet again in the evenings. They took long walks through the dark city streets, as gusts of wind swirled the dry autumn leaves around them. Or they strolled through the nearby woods, gradually en- veloped by the wintry silence. "Strange," thinks Trank, "how we never ran out of things to talk about." Later in the evening, he would bring Maria home. She lived with her parents in a middle-class neighborhood; he lived with his mother in a working-class neighbor- hood all the way across town. And after midnight, after the last trains and buses had already passed, he would walk home – a journey of one and a half hours – through the cold and lifeless city, absolutely glowing, feeling so alive.

On these nights, he scarcely needed any sleep. He found himself in a constant state of excitement. This whole time, though, he hardly ever actually slept with Maria. What had been an integral part of their lives in the south of France was now precluded by the puritanical atmosphere in her home, with only a few exceptions. But this issue was not even really so important to him. It was all about winning over this girl's heart. Everything else was insignificant.

Trank had left behind what was conventionally deemed to be "reality" (the things that keep people busy, the things one hears about in the news each day.) Instead, he had started living in his own personal reality. His life took on an entirely different quality than ever before – or ever since.

The rest of his daily life was experienced as if from afar. The usual day-to-day activities played only a secondary role. It didn't matter to him whether he ate, or slept, or worked, or kept up-to-date on what was happening in the world.

He neglected his mother (a fact about which she complained bitterly) as well as his friends, and did only the bare minimum at the Institute. When Wickler stepped into his office shortly before lunchtime, and – as was his habit – attempted to enter into some long, convoluted discussion right at that particular moment, Trank did not hesitate to end the conversation as soon as the clock struck noon. "Professor, I apologize," he said, "but I have an appointment and I need to leave." Without even awaiting a reply, he grabbed his coat and was out the door, leaving Wickler staring after him in bewilderment.

Later, after he finally married Maria, this invigorating courage disappeared. He would never dare to do such a thing again, as he gradually settled into the life of a responsible adult.

The only possible reason for this was that he had achieved his goal, that he had accomplished his only purpose in life – and so he now began living an aimless, purposeless existence. So now he must be in need of a new purpose. He will have to set a new goal for himself. He needs a North Star to guide him, to facilitate his primordial essence in breaking through the barrier of his daily routine.

Thinking back on his conquest of Maria, he has no doubt that part of his very essence is the priceless relationship that he has with his wife and the children. They obviously mean a lot to him. He admits, though, that in the last few years he has somewhat grown apart from them.

And it is only he himself who is doing this estranging. They seek him out; he seals himself off. They try to have him take part in their joys and achievements, and he responds dismissively, if at all.

This must also be one of the reasons why Maria has been so discreet in the ways she worries over him – it is because he clearly can't handle her direct questions, instead just irritatedly brushing them off.

His relatively well-mannered children look to him for guidance. Instead, as he now realizes, he usually offers them only cynical remarks. It happens when they ask him about some current event, or what he thinks about some movie, or anything of the sort.

"I've been blocking out the people who are closest to me," Trank observes regretfully, "just the same way that I have been blocking out my own self. This is absolutely ludicrous. In the exact place where I can truly make a difference – and my family is just waiting for me to do so – I am an utter failure, unable to see something truly important amid the plethora of unimportant things in my everyday life. And in fact, my life is not even all that hectic."

* * *

The chairman claps his hands and announces that the meeting will proceed. The board members all sit up and turn to face him. "I notice, though," he continues, the right corner of his mouth curving upwards slightly, "that our second secretary seems to be rather absent today. He is probably contemplating problems that are more important than those that we are discussing in this meeting. Judging by the persistent frown on his face, he must be worrying about nothing less than the long-term future of the foundation."

Brockstätte casts him a punitive look, as the board members break out in hearty laughter. A smirk even creeps onto Hartmann's lips. Trank tries to find an appropriate expression; a poker face is the only thing that would be appropriate, but he doesn't succeed in pulling one off. His face muscles refuse to obey his will; they involuntarily contort themselves in such a way that his jaw is clenched shut and his cheekbones quiver.

The important thing is not even so much the fact that he is being victimized, but the fact that the board members can just laugh so relaxedly while he sits there so tense. The question is, though, how can they remain so aloof, while he cannot? And he realizes that it is because they never sully themselves by getting personally involved in matters, instead having everything done by subordinates whom they control. Trank, though, would like to be able to have this aloofness while still remaining involved, solidly grounded and deeply entrenched in reality.

A picture, one that he has pinned up on the wall at home, pops into his head. It is a picture of a lone, twisted pine, clutching to the rock above the treeline in California's Sierra Nevada Mountains. Its roots, in their quest for water, penetrate deep into the cracks in the rocks; they intertwine, striving for greater stability. Although exposed to the elements, the tree remains defiant. Courageous. Independent. Focused on the essential. Hungry for life.

This symbol, though, does not correspond to the board members at all. They are rather more like birds of prey that land on the tree in order to scope out the area. Should he, in fact, strive for a career like the careers of the board members? A life like those birds of prey, rather than like the tree? His reflections from this morning have not quite ruled out this path, if he should want to follow it.

Impetuous Trank immediately says no; the tree in the Sierra Nevadas stands aloof just fine, with a wide-open perspective over a vast domain. And, Rational Trank adds, something inside me ultimately led me to study history, choosing to occupy my time with theories rather than actions. I have long ago rejected the notion that I would exercise some sort of power to shape the world according to my own will, to mold it to serve my own ends, to put my mark on it, to build something up on the backs of others.

Has any such career, based on power and wealth and prestige, ever had a more profound meaning? Well, perhaps if it led to immortality on the basis of glorious deeds, as the Romans believed.

But it is a lot more difficult to immortalize oneself in such a way nowadays, in an era of mass production and systemization. Fewer and fewer people truly qualify as being exceptional. Even famous thinkers and artists and scientists now emerge en masse, and produce en masse within accepted paradigms – to say nothing of the way managers and politicians work.

Trank eyes the men sitting around the table, and feels no desire to become a part of their illustrious circle, to join them in patting each other on the back appreciatively for the rest of their lives.

* * *

A look around the room reveals that an edgy mood has suddenly crept in. The jovial atmosphere from earlier is gone.

Kindlimann has just asked Oederlein, "Would you be so kind as to curtail your smoking? The stench from your cigarettes is appalling, and it has become unbearable."

Berglass seizes the opportunity to declare, "You know, it is out of respect for my fellow men, amongst other reasons, that I smoke only a pipe. My experience tells me that most people actually appreciate its tangy scent – though if that is not the case here, then I can certainly abstain."

"Your scholarly pipe is not the subject of discussion here," snarls Oederlein, who then turns to Kindlimann. "I may smoke, but at least I don't booze." Kindlimann turns white and looks to von Warteck for support. Von Warteck remains silent, refusing to get involved.

"For as long as I am in charge here," the chairman interjects, "I intend to run all meetings in such a way that all participants feel comfortable. So I kindly request you, Mr. Kindlimann, to please change seats, ideally towards the foot of the table, so that Mr. Oederlein's and Professor Berglass' smoke do not bother you. Mr. Trank shall refrain from smoking."

* * *

Slowly Trank is beginning to see things clearer. It is all still bewilderingly new, and it is not exactly something he could summarize in a few words. But he is definitely in the process of zeroing in on what he wants. And a sort of ground rule is beginning to emerge, which calls for him to live a life that flows naturally along with time, thus developing a feel for the steady passage of time. Only in this manner can he determine whether he is utilizing his allotted lifespan properly.

What this ultimately means is that, as soon as he is assured of being able to provide for his basic needs, then it is time itself that will matter – not money. Time, which he can use to draw something out of himself that undoubtedly exists within him – even if it is buried quite deeply.

"Traitor!" Impetuous Trank retorts impulsively. "If you start thinking that way about the meaning of life, you'll end up wiping away all the values that your proletarian family instilled in you."

In his family, life was to be lived quietly to oneself, along predetermined paths. Any greater challenges were shunned. Life was undemanding; it unfolded rather pleasantly, with very little intensity. High-intensity lifestyles were reserved for heroes and leaders – athletes, movie stars, politicians, industrialists, the kinds of people they would see on television and read about in the newspapers.

Trank's parents and other relatives were content to follow the adventures of such important people vicariously. At best, they perhaps dreamed of such careers for their offspring.

It was exactly for this reason that Trank's parents had made is possible for him to go to university. For his now-dead father, second secretary at FPHI would have been more than acceptable as a career pinnacle. He would have been unable to understand why Trank was not happy with it. He would have talked end-lessly, like a broken record, about how nice it was to enjoy such prestige and such a decent salary.

Trank suddenly recalls one of his childhood friends, also the son of a blue-collar worker. The two of them would play together with their plastic action figures, which they had acquired by collecting chewing gum wrappers. Trank always assumed that each of them would want as many action figures (i.e., power, wealth, prestige) as possible to himself, and that the toys should thus be divided up equally. His friend, though, apparently quite wise despite his young age, just smiled and let Trank have most of the action figures. At the same time, the stories that this friend made up while playing were actually more interesting.

Trank regrets the fact that he has not yet mastered the art of renunciation. As the example from his youth illustrates, such renunciation may involve a sacrifice at the start, but later opens up possibilities that easily make up for this.

If he wants to grasp the essential, then he must learn to renounce that which is glamorous but non-essential. The line that says "what is essential is invisible to the eye" echoes in his mind, but catchphrases are not what he needs right now. On to the task at hand.

From now on, it will be a matter of taking everything that distracts him from the important things in life and casting such things aside as deadweight. So, what does he absolutely, unconditionally need?

He needs food, shelter, a safe place to rest his head at night, and some form of sexual release. Then he needs his familial support system, some means of self-affirmation, and presumably social relationships. He definitely must also have culture in his life – a notion he internalized over the course of his studies. And, as the foundation of it all, a way to provide the basics – and only the basics – for himself and his family.

During all his ruminations this entire morning, he has not yet thought about his social relationships.

As soon as he does, a sense of disgust comes over him. These relationships are only rarely substantive. It is no wonder, given the fact that the very lives of his acquaintances lack substance, as does his own. There simply is not a whole lot to talk about, beyond the usual chitchat about what is going on at work or at home. It is a pity that they waste their emotions on it. And even when one of them experiences something that is truly worth relishing, he is jealously drowned out or silenced by someone who thinks himself more important.

Trank recalls how, once during a coffee break, Miss Derring asked him something about the Minotaur. Trank, as a historian familiar with Cretan mythology, launched into an explanation. But he was brutally interrupted by Brockstätte, who started babbling on about his vacation in Crete. Brockstätte's tone made it clear that since Trank could not have visited the island as he had, the only one qualified to expound on it was he himself. Everything he said sounded artificial though. "He's parroting some guidebook," thought Trank. "He did not truly experience the place."

Now Trank asks himself whether his contemporaries ever truly experience the world. It seems like things really only happen on television and in the newspapers. The insignificant tidbits of information they exchange over coffee or lunch tend to come directly from the mouths of these two-dimensional figures on the television screen, and they relate to world events from the last few days at most. During these conversations, Trank's own views often clash with popular opinion, especially when he, the historian, is being lectured about historical events as they supposedly play out in reality, not in the dusty scholarly books. His friends and acquaintances, though, no longer seek to acquire human knowledge in a discerning and critical manner, instead choosing to believe in whatever comes easily and suits them – even things as silly as astrology.

Gone are the university days, gone are the hours dedicated to discussing ideas. And even when a meaningful topic somehow does come up around the table nowadays, it is inevitably treated in a very impersonal manner; the people do not say what they actually feel, instead saying only what they think they are supposed to say. Between their souls and their tongues are a myriad of filters that censor and distort everything.

The only thing substantive which Trank can grab onto in these situations is the food. And the wine. He wolfs down his throat as much of this "substance" as he can, and drinks way more of it than he should. Fortunately, he does not tend to gain weight, though all of this does regularly make him feel sick.

* * *

While Trank is contemplating what form his social contacts will take in the future, he is once again pulled back to the reality of the meeting. And he is not even caught off-guard – after twenty-six meetings, he is capable of indulging in his thoughts while simultaneously following the meeting with half an ear.

Von Warteck is proposing financial support for up-and-coming young members of the parties represented in the current national government. He is standing beside the projection screen with a telescopic pointer that he has pulled from his breast pocket, and is teetering on his feet impatiently. The chairman summons Trank to stand by the projector and display the relevant slides as per von Warteck's instructions.

Trank hates the fact that his thoughts have been interrupted right at this very moment, right when he is in the process of finally getting a handle on his future. He is not the least bit interested in von Warteck's strategy for protecting the political elite. He is interested only in his own strategy for getting away from this nonsense.

The disruption of his planning only cements his decision. He must act now. "Today, this very day," says Impetuous Trank. "You've made a promise."

Von Warteck's presentation takes a full twenty minutes and is completely superfluous, since it is entirely obvious from the start that the proposal will be approved. With so much money flowing into the foundation, it is glad to find projects that can be backed unhesitatingly. Not even Hartmann will be against this one; the party he supports, thanks to constant mismanagement, suffers from a chronic lack of funds.

Trank wonders whether all of the slides that von Warteck presents to the other boards of directors on which he sits are as meaningless as these. He must admit that the CEO has a generous enough staff of employees just like he himself, who, lacking any better goals in life, are probably able to spend all their time carefully tailoring each of their boss' presentations to each individual board.

After the presentation, something occurs which Trank had not been expecting: Berglass and Kindlimann insist upon discussing the matter further. They will not just plainly approve the proposal; they must ornately embellish their endorsement. They talk as if cameras are pointed at them.

What a shame that Professor Zurzinger is no longer on the board. On these sorts of occasions, he would brusquely interrupt, quite loudly declaring that his time was valuable and that he needed to get back to his zoological laboratory. If it was clear that everyone was in agreement, then further discussion was unnecessary; the chairman should simply put the matter to a vote already.

He was ignored by the other board members, who would not allow themselves to be lectured by the professor. Zurzinger responded by starting to appear at the meetings for two hours only, as he felt this was sufficient time to cover all the items on the agenda. Eventually the board would put up with him no longer, and the chairman suggested he resign. He did so immediately and (as he wrote) with satisfaction. In keeping with the board's adherence to the principles of consociational democracy, Professor Berglass was then hired to succeed him as the board's representative from the academic world.

* * *

While Impetuous Trank is outraged by the board's time-consuming exercises, Rational Trank tries to see things differently. Maybe the relationship between von Warteck and his colleagues is something like that between a novelist and his readers. The mere words alone are not enough; the reader of the novel must use his imagination to bring those words to life; likewise, von Warteck's colleagues probably see more meaning in his words than Trank is capable of seeing. He simply lacks the antennae necessary to receive the broadcast at its full strength, or perhaps the sensorium to process it – just like the board members are probably incapable of grasping the novels that Trank himself reads.

After all, Rational Trank admits, much of the meeting has a certain ritualistic character. And he has become convinced that human enterprises, if nothing comes in their way, will generally have certain self-reinforcing tendencies that function almost as ends unto themselves.

The foundation, for example, basically only serves itself.

Its founder, a certain Ferdinand Hablützel (of whom the foundation's lawyer is a direct descendant) had dedicated himself to counteracting the inherent jinx in the German meaning of his name – which implied that he would "have little" in life. He raked in tons of money in the cocoa bean trade around the start of the nineteenth century. He was childless and starting to get on in years when he met the humanitarian Henri Dunant, and was so impressed with the man that he decided to bequeath his entire fortune for the advancement of humanism.

It could be, Trank reflects, that the money was put to efficient and effective use at the time. But these days, the foundation would not really be missed at all. Its original purpose no longer suffices to render it meaningful. Consequently, it makes use of administrative extravagance to give the impression of meaningful activity – for example, the quarterly reports that Trank prepares exclusively for the archive. And it weaves an increasingly complex web of rules for the processing of applications.

But who could ever convince the chairman, the board members, or Brockstätte of the meaninglessness of their activities? They would defend everything vehemently. Neither the foundation's stated purpose nor its bylaws can be questioned, nor can the nature of its dealings, as long as they comply with the bylaws. And ultimately, they would say, a traditional institution that has survived for one hundred and fifty years possesses a certain inherent value, in and of itself.

Trank begins to suspect that the inertia that has frozen him in place, the inertia that has caused him to just drift haphazardly for years within the confines of his routine, corresponds to the inertia of the foundation itself.

"Then it's really high time we break away!" insists Impetuous Trank.

"Break away to where? To what?" asks Rational Trank.

If he had no responsibilities, no obligations, no bonds, then he would love to just head straight for the Canadian wilderness. He would live there as simply as possible, with only the basics. He would build a log cabin amidst the fragrant pines, dig a well, plant a vegetable garden in a clearing, go hunting and fishing, teach his children how to live in the wilderness.

But he is not quite ready for this. Not only because his years in academia were not exactly the best possible way to prepare for a lifetime in the wilderness, but also because such a lifestyle would require an immediate total commitment from him, burying all of his own personal interests beneath a layer of pine needles.

So where then?

Finally it becomes clear to him. As usual, he has not reached the answer directly; he has approached it in a roundabout manner, craftily moving about as if it were all one big chess match, constantly probing and rejecting every possible alternative course. The whole process started two months ago, but only now does he finally see things distinctly. He recognizes that he has been blundering about aimlessly for years. He knows where and when it all began – on Belle-Île.

And the only way out? He must go back to that very same place – as if at that very same time – and start over once again.

* * *

One summery Sunday two months ago, Maria's brother, the civil engineer, popped in for a visit. The kids were out at the neighborhood swimming pool. Trank sat with Maria and her brother in the comfortable garden chairs, as the three of them sipped coffee beneath the awning. They chatted quietly, as nature dozed away languidly in the heat around them. A reddish tinge of sunlight permeated his closed eyelids.

Without Trank even realizing it, his brother-in-law shifted the conversation to his work. He needed to organize files containing several years worth of project documents, and he also wanted to set up a small technical library for himself and his nine and a half employees. His company's expensive reference works and journals and handbooks kept getting lost beneath the mountains of papers that had accumulated around the office, and he could not go on like this any longer. And finally, he wanted to transform his company into a stock corporation, and he needed assistance with this as well.

The words, muffled by the hazy heat, were reaching Trank's ears only faintly up until this moment. But then came the upshot: if Trank were to finally decide that he had had enough of working at the foundation, then he could start work with his brother-in-law anytime.

Of course, Trank was flabbergasted. And, with an insecure laugh, he immediately replied that the offer must be some sort of joke. "No, not at all," his brother-in-law assured him, sounding slightly annoyed.

Maria asked about the possible salary. The number her brother mentioned was about half of what Trank was earning at FPHI. But Trank would really be able to take it easy there, he said.

Maria then expressed her concerns regarding their mortgage. Her brother suggested that they sell their house and move somewhere nearby his own home. Their tiny townhouse, with its tiny yard, didn't really offer them anything more than a nice spacious apartment would offer them anyway, he said. And he could even help hook them up with an affordable place.

And on it went; there was a solution for every potential problem. Maria's brother had clearly thought everything through quite systematically already. Trank suddenly felt very unsure. Was he really unhappy? If he were to take up his brother-in-law's offer, what improvement would there actually be in his life?

He sidestepped the questions, jokingly painting an exaggerated image of the future. He himself breeding rabbits, Maria farming chickens, becoming self-subsistent – after his ruminations today, those thoughts did not even seem so absurd anymore. Maria and her brother played along, evidently for his sake. The three of them built ludicrous castles in the sky and shared some hearty laughs.

His brother-in-law reiterated while leaving, though, that the offer remained open – it was up to Trank to accept it, and the sooner the better.

* * *

Meanwhile, Kindlimann is going all out to express his support for a traveling exhibition about the history of the Swiss cavalry. The otherwise listless ex-general is now bursting with enthusiasm. And of course, as usual, he does not fail to reaffirm his position that the dissolution of this noble branch of the military was a regrettably bad decision on the part of the nation's politicians.

The board will unanimously approve this project as well. Trank will subsequently prepare a letter to the one who had requested it, and will submit this letter for the chairman's signature along with the corresponding excerpt of the meeting minutes. He relishes the thought of avoiding such an apparently important task.

Slowly, a broad outline of his future begins to emerge.

He needs a simple, concrete profession, one which is geared towards immediately recognizable goals rather than towards empty procedures. He must be doing things that clearly need to get done – whether gardening or farming or nursing or auto repair or even accounting if absolutely necessary. Otherwise, he will get stuck in the same old rut of undertaking stressful work only to serve others, while constantly struggling against the powerful routines that are embedded in such jobs. The offer from his brother-in-law can thus be accepted for only a short period at most; the nature of his work would be too similar to what it is now at the foundation, just perhaps a bit more friendly.

It is not yet quite clear to him how he will manage to get into a suitable profession. What is clear, though, is that it must leave him enough time for his own creative pursuits. Some visionary personal project perhaps, one that supersedes the minutiae of daily life – maybe something historical.

He has more than enough ideas. A door is pushed

open somewhere inside his mind at this very moment, and the ideas come pouring through it once again. Complex, mysterious, intricate worlds, just waiting for him to decipher them.

He vows not to undertake anything in his future life that is motivated by fame or fortune – otherwise his situation would again resemble his current situation at the foundation. Instead, he will pursue his historical research for his own edification, with complete freedom and autonomy – after all, not everything a man does must be done for the sake of societal progress.

These goals are worth the relinquishment of his higher salary, of his prestigious position as second secretary at FPHI, and even of the small townhouse. And, if necessary, he would even sacrifice the Saab, the only pride he has left on those weary evenings sitting in the crush of rush-hour traffic. He is ready to follow this path.

"But if we only take up Maria's brother's offer for a short period of time, what comes next?" asks Rational Trank. "Would we subsequently be able to leave the security of that job, without something else already in hand?"

"Come on," pleads Impetuous Trank, "don't start getting insecure again after we've come so far! Just put your fears aside for once. Now is when we take our big step out into the unknown!"

Rational Trank still hesitates. "This is a very fundamental decision being taken today. It is all so shocking to the system. Maybe we should sleep on it one last time."

"No, this sort of procrastination is unacceptable!" exclaims Impetuous Trank. "Nothing will ever get done this way. I fully intend to get us off this wrong path. I have a good feeling about this, and the best part is that we can get started right away! Look, after all these wasted years, I want to get this done as soon as possible, and I'm sure that we can find a better solution; we just need to actually start seeking it. After such a long paralysis, we need to get moving!"

"I realize this," Rational Trank admits, "and I also notice that, when it comes to these sorts of decisions, I always win out over you with my careful consideration of all relevant factors – and yet this has not prevented us from getting tangled up in the thicket of boredom for all these years. So now the moment has come for me to rely on you and your instincts. It is only now that I grasp this. Nothing will change if I continue to stay within my comfort zone – things can change only if I deliver myself to the unknown and trust in my own creativity."

Trank finally sees clearly and unequivocally what must be done, and feels a wave of happiness – a long-buried happiness – spread through him once again.

* * *

The end of the meeting is gradually approaching. The board members, as is their tradition, will go out to eat together. Oederlein and Kindlimann will resolve their dispute amicably over lunch. It is all part of the process.

One important item is left on the agenda – the board's autumn excursion. Trank is certain that they will spend the entire remaining half-hour discussing it. Berglass will suggest a stopover at a monastery, Kindlimann tastings at a winery, von Warteck a trip to the mountains of Graubünden, Oederlein a tour of some industrial enterprise, and Hartmann a visit to the Swiss Federal Railways' newest signal tower.

But Trank can wait no longer.

He stands up, steps over between Biland and Brockstätte and loudly announces, "Gentlemen, unfortunately I must attend to a private matter immediately. I suggest that Mr. Brockstätte take over the meeting minutes from here; as first secretary, he can certainly handle it."

Silence suddenly reigns in the room. Everyone just stares at him, obviously finding his behavior horrifically inappropriate.

Brockstätte goes pale. Biland bitingly declares, "Either sit down immediately or give me a legitimate reason why you must go – but I warn you: if it is not a genuine emergency, then you are in very hot water."

"What a rotten lazy dog," mutters Kindlimann.

"Judging by your smell, it's you who's rotten," Trank calmly replies. Berglass and Hartmann laugh, and even Oederlein's mouth curves upward slightly. "What gall!" exclaims von Warteck. "In our company that would be grounds for immediate termination!"

"But this is not your company, Mr. Warteck." says Trank. " So you're not in charge here."

"Please bring this meeting to order, Mr. Chairman," gasps Oederlein, half-rising from his seat, "or I shall leave immediately!"

"So demands Mr. Oederlein, member of the National Council, always a stickler for order," jibes Trank. This time it is Kindlimann who bursts out laughing, while Hartmann and Berglass just grin.

Biland is repeatedly rapping his silver pen against the table, quite forcefully. "Quiet! Quiet please!" he shouts, red-faced. "Let me speak!"

Trank grins at him. "But Mr. Chairman," he says, "you usually keep your cool much better than this – please spare your nerves. And, by the way, you're destroying this expensive table with your pen. No need to react this way over a lowly second secretary..."

Brockstätte jumps up and wedges himself protectively in front of Biland, who screams, "You're fired! Effective immediately! What a disgrace! Get out of here right now!"

"Ah, well, I've already quit, effective immediately," replies Trank, as he tosses the president a folded sheet of paper on which he had enthusiastically jotted down a quick resignation letter, just moments before he stood up. He had even noted the exact time. As he reaches the door, he looks back one last time and says, "Gentlemen, that's all. My work here is done; you can hold your applause. Farewell then."

Biland has turned his chair towards the door, and Brockstätte remains by the chairman's side. Everyone stares incredulously. He will remember them all exactly like this.

* * *

It had been a long time since Trank had enjoyed anything as much as he enjoyed this. Laughing out loud, he heads towards his office two floors below. He looks at the files on his desk with disgust, thinking of the hundreds of superfluous and meaningless details contained within them, of the endless repetition – most of which is purely to comply with formalities. The paperwork that could never be finished – the files flowed onto his desk each day at least as fast as he could process them.

There are just a few personal things inside and on top of the desk. He pulls a plastic bag from a drawer and tosses them inside. He takes down a photo of jazz musicians that he had snapped on 42nd Street in New York, placing it neatly into his briefcase. Finally, he dials his home phone number.

Maria picks up immediately. "Hi, dear," he says cheerfully, "how's everything at home? What are you doing now?"

"Well, I'm in the kitchen of course – but tell me, why do you sound so bouncy?"

"Oh, I'm just bouncing around the office, clearing it out – the rest of our life comes next."

"Are you kidding? What's going on?"

"Listen," he says calmly, "I just dropped a bomb-shell here and got myself dismissed, effective immediately. Sorry this had to happen so suddenly, but there was no other way. Anyway, I feel so much better than I have felt in a very, very long time. And I promise you, I will do everything I can to find myself a new job as soon as possible, even if it's just working for your brother."

It is as if he has just slapped Maria; he does not know whether she will cry or snap back at him. But instead, she answers just as calmly as him, "You know, I'm less surprised than you probably think. The children and I have known for quite a while that you weren't doing well; we saw your unhappiness from a distance, but we were stuck just racking our brains trying to figure out what we could possibly do. But now that you've taken the first step, we can plan the rest of it together."

"That is the best gift that you and the children could possibly give me," Trank says, as he feels a certain confidence spreading through him. "I have just one more wish now."

"What is it?"

"Instead of Tuscany, I want to go back to Belle-Île for our summer vacation – back to where things first got dragged off-course. I want to start again from there."

"I'm definitely okay with that, and I'm sure that the kids will be as well. When will you be home?"

"I'm coming right now – at this admittedly quite unusual hour."

Gerold Trank then leaves his office without looking back. He feels exhilarated. He feels adventurous. Trying to whistle a complicated jazz tune, he heads down the stairs, past the quarters of the caretaker (who calls out to him, staring in puzzlement as he strides by), and out into the bright sunshine.